Sam stood in the doorway, his hands hooked loosely on his hips

The way the light hit his gold b⋯⋯⋯⋯⋯⋯e like a beacon of goo⋯⋯⋯⋯ thought. The loo⋯⋯⋯⋯ was anything but ⋯⋯⋯⋯ her feel kind of—

Well. There was no ⋯⋯⋯⋯. Either her new aphrodisiac tea recipe was starting to work way faster than she'd thought it would, or Sam's nearness was about to bring her supreme satisfaction. And although Rosie knew her teas were good, she was pragmatic enough to realize they weren't *that* good.

"Um, hi, chief," she said, gripping her mug tightly with both hands to keep herself from grabbing his shirt and ripping it off. "I'm actually not open yet…." It was a struggle to get the words out. The next time she brewed a batch of this tea, she definitely needed to be in a different ZIP code than Sam. Or maybe a different area code. Or country. Or hemisphere. Or galaxy. Yeah, that might be enough.

"That's okay," Sam told her, though the look he was giving her was anything but okay.

In fact, that look made her think his reason for showing up here was, oh…Rosie didn't know… to have really smokin' sex.

Dear Reader,

Having grown up in a fairly metropolitan city, I've always been fascinated by small towns and small-town life. When I was a kid, I gravitated toward shows like *Petticoat Junction* and *Green Acres* and *Mayberry, RFD,* because I loved the humor generated by situations where the sense of worldly innocence was so over-the-top.

When I decided to site *My Only Vice* in a small town, I naturally thought about those shows again, but with a more, um, adult sensibility this time. Yes, I'm talking about the sexual aspect of those small towns. I mean, there must have *been* a sexual aspect, right? Opie didn't just appear out of thin air, ya know. But Sam and Rosie, both products of the big city transplanted to cozy Northaven, Massachusetts, can't help but bring their clichéd notions of innocent small-town life with them.

Which makes for great fun when they realize small-town life can be a lot steamier than they thought....

Happy reading!

Elizabeth Bevarly

ELIZABETH
BEVARLY
My Only Vice

HARLEQUIN®

TORONTO • NEW YORK • LONDON
AMSTERDAM • PARIS • SYDNEY • HAMBURG
STOCKHOLM • ATHENS • TOKYO • MILAN • MADRID
PRAGUE • WARSAW • BUDAPEST • AUCKLAND

ISBN-13: 978-0-373-79277-1
ISBN-10:   0-373-79277-8

MY ONLY VICE

ABOUT THE AUTHOR

Elizabeth Bevarly is the *New York Times* bestselling, RITA®Award–nominated author of more than fifty novels and eight novellas. Although she grew up in a fairly large city, she now resides in a small town that boasts only one retail establishment. Fortunately, it also boasts one restaurant—which comes in very handy when she's on deadline.

Books by Elizabeth Bevarly

HARLEQUIN BLAZE
189—INDECENT SUGGESTION

HARLEQUIN FLIPSIDE
25—UNDERCOVER WITH THE MOB

HQN BOOKS
EXPRESS MALE
YOU'VE GOT MALE

SILHOUETTE DESIRE
1363—THE TEMPTATION OF RORY MONAHAN
1389—WHEN JAYNE MET ERIK
1406—THE SECRET LIFE OF CONNOR MONAHAN
1474—TAMING THE PRINCE
1501—TAMING THE BEASTLY MD

For David
My Only Love

1

As HE WATCHED the seemingly endless parade of nearly naked, thoroughly sweaty female torsos gyrating wildly to electronic funk music, it occurred to Sam Maguire that small-town life wasn't exactly what he'd expected it to be. Of course, the reason for this particular parade of naked, sweaty female torsos *wasn't* to earn its owners a living, however dubious, which would have likely been the case for such a display in the big city. No, the reason for this particular parade of naked, sweaty torsos was more to keep its owners in shape—however dubious.

That was beside the point.

The point was that a naked, sweaty female torso was a naked, sweaty female torso, and it was a sight to be revered, whether under the strobe lights of Buster's Bootie Call in Boston, or under the Art Deco fixtures of Alice's Aerobics Attic in tiny Northaven, two hours away. So Sam would, by God, revere them. Even the ones at Alice's that hadn't quite gotten around to that in-shape thing yet. Hell, it wasn't as if the bodies at Buster's were exactly ready for their close-up. The tattoos on most of them had headed farther south than Tierra del Fuego.

Sam's reason for watching these torsos, however, *wasn't* much different from what his reason for watching them in the big city had been. A stakeout was a stakeout, too, whether it was in Boston or Northaven, even if the criminal element here consisted less of drug pushers and vicious pimps and more of dognappers and petty thieves. Even at that, Mrs. Pendleton's Yorkie had turned up safe and sound by nightfall just as Sam had assured the elderly woman it would, and she never received one of the animal's red beribboned little ears along with a ransom note, as Mrs. Pendleton had been so certain she would. The local thefts were no more difficult to solve than the isolated dognapping had been, since most of those were perpetrated by fresh-faced teenagers who didn't even know enough to hide their tracks, so unaccustomed were they to a life of crime.

Sam's current case was easily the ugliest he'd investigated since his self-inflicted relocation to Northaven a little over a year ago. Alice the aerobics instructor's estranged husband had been drinking too much white Zinfandel on the weekends and making threatening phone calls to her. But his crime, too, was a far cry from similar ones committed in the big city, since the worst of Don's threats had been to spend with wild abandon, using the joint MasterCard he and Alice still shared. To the tune of *five hundred dollars* if Alice didn't give him a second chance to make up for his indiscretion with the head cashier at his grocery store.

Nevertheless, Sam had promised Alice he would stop by both her house and the aerobics business on his daily rounds to make sure Don didn't try anything funny.

Well, anything funnier than racking up a three-figure debt on a credit card, anyway. So what if Sam lingered at the latter destination a little longer than he did the former? Alice's business was open to the public, and was therefore more easily accessible than her home. And her customer base constituted a threat to more people than just Alice herself. Any cop, urban *or* small town, would make sure he lingered longer in the more open—and consequently more ripe for mayhem—environment.

Especially if that was the environment that had the naked, sweaty, gyrating female torsos. Talk about your mayhem…

The women in Alice's current class didn't know Sam was watching them, since Alice had instructed him to enter through the back and observe the studio from behind the wall of two-way glass, just in case he arrived at a time when Don was indeed there trying to wreak havoc. Presumably by doing something crazy like waving around a loaded Juiceman he'd just flagrantly purchased with their credit card—and not on sale, either. But as Sam's gaze roved down the line of women and he recognized one of them as Rosie Bliss, he was in an even smaller hurry to leave.

Northaven's resident florist had her lush fall of dark red hair—hair that normally tumbled to nearly the center of her back—piled loosely atop her head, held in place by some invisible means of support. She was wearing a clingy yellow…whatever the hell you called those things women worked out in that barely covered their breasts…over clingy black…whatever the hell you called those things women worked out in that barely covered their asses. Every other inch of her was creamy, ivory—and sweaty; did he mention sweaty? And gyrating, too?—flesh. She was even working out barefoot, unlike the other women, who were all wearing sneakers, and something about the way her toenails were painted a dark blood red made Sam want to...

Well. There was no way he could deny it. He wanted to suck on Rosie Bliss's toes until the cows came home. Then he wanted to suck on the rest of her until the cows went out again. And he'd hope like hell they never brought their bovine little selves back again.

Sam had had his first run-in with Rosie the day he'd arrived in sleepy Northaven feeling messed up and beaten down by his final case in Boston—the one that had made him look for a job in a place like sleepy Northaven. Of course, Sam had had a run-in with just about everyone in town that day a year ago this past September, including the mayor and the head of Northaven College, the town's reason for existence. Hell, practically the entire population of Northaven had turned out to greet their new Chief of Police that day—with a picnic in the park, no less.

But it had been Rosie, with that lush fall of dark red hair and those incredible green eyes and that body that leaped right off a trifold with staples, whom Sam had taken home with him that night. She'd been the one who'd joined him in his bed after dark for hours and hours of the downest, most dirtiest sex he'd ever enjoyed.

Not literally, of course, since he'd realized within moments of making Rosie's acquaintance that she was way too nice a woman for something like hours and hours of down and dirty sex, especially with a guy she'd just met. But Sam wasn't too nice for that. As evidenced by the fact that he'd gone home after meeting the nicest woman he'd ever met in his life and fantasized for hours and hours about having down and dirty sex with her.

Hey, it had been a while at that point since he'd had *any* sex with *any*one, all right? Not that he'd had much sex *since* meeting Rosie, either—or *any* sex since meeting her…dammit—because Northaven was so overrun with damned nice women. He still had better sex with his fantasy Rosie Bliss than he'd ever had with any flesh-and-blood woman. So he had sex with his fantasy Rosie Bliss *a lot.*

But it was absolutely essential that he keep his distance from the flesh-and-blood Rosie Bliss. Especially the flesh part of her. The last thing he needed or wanted in his life was a nice woman. Not much in Sam's life had ever been nice. He didn't do nice. He didn't want nice. And he sure as hell didn't deserve nice. Even if there was a part of him that still craved it in the form of Rosie Bliss.

He told himself it was time to leave Alice's Aerobics Attic since, clearly, there was nothing amiss at the studio. But he couldn't quite make himself look away from Rosie. Her gaze was fixed on the part of the mirror that was in front of her, a few feet away from where Sam stood. Almost without realizing he was doing it, he moved down until he was standing right in front of her, so that it felt as if she was looking at him, instead of her reflection.

There. That was better. Maybe it wasn't him making

Rosie gyrate and sweat the way she was, but there was nothing wrong with pretending it was him, right? Aside from the fact that it made him seem like a pathetic loser, he meant.

Ah, screw it. As long as nobody else found out that he, whose nickname at Boston Vice had been Ironheart, was lusting after a goody-two-shoes florist in a place so saccharine it would make Norman Rockwell gag, Sam was in the clear. He'd defy any heterosexual male *not* to succumb to the charms of Rosie Bliss. And even the gay ones would have lusted after her flair for flower arrangement.

The electronic funk music on the other side of the mirror segued into something slower and less frenetic, so the movement of the women became slower and less frenetic, too. Sam continued to watch Rosie as she stretched her arms up high and brought them down again in two graceful arcs, pushing them behind her back and linking them together before thrusting her chest forward. When she did that, the clingy yellow…whatever the hell you called those things women worked out in…stretched taut, defining two ample, exquisite breasts whose nipples pushed through the fabric without an ounce of inhibition. His fingers twitched involuntarily at the sight, as did another part of his anatomy that had no business twitching while he was on the cock…uh, clock. Try as he might, though, he simply could not make himself look away.

Not for the first time, he wondered why she was living in Northaven. He'd learned shortly after meeting her that she'd moved to town less than a year before he had. Even though their paths had crossed scarcely a dozen times since, usually at meetings of the Northaven Business Owners' Guild or some kind of civic function or holiday celebration, he'd spoken with her often enough to form the impression that her origins weren't as small town as her current life was. No one in Northaven seemed to know a lot about her—except that she was extremely nice to everyone and didn't have a mean bone in her incredibly luscious body. And also that she was an absolute whiz with snapdragons.

Maybe she'd been driven to Northaven for reasons similar to his own, Sam thought as he watched her arc one arm over her head and bend her entire body to the side in a position he was sure would make for interesting coupling. Of course, as far as he was concerned, when it came to Rosie, sorting the laundry would make for interesting coupling. As would sweeping out the garage. And grocery shopping. Retrieving the mail. Hosing out the garbage cans…

He was about to indulge in his favorite Rosie fantasy—the one where he hired her to do a little, uh, landscaping on his, um, enormous oak—when the front door to Alice's Aerobics Attic opened and her husband, Don, walked in. Although it was Alice's name he called out, every woman in the room turned to look at him. Sam, too—very reluctantly—tore his gaze from Rosie and turned his attention to the other man.

Don looked even worse now than he'd looked the last time Sam saw him. His green Clover Mart jacket was rumpled, and the brisk early-October wind had blown his salt-and-pepper comb-over completely off the top of his head without his even having noticed it. He seemed a lot older than his fifty-eight years, which Sam supposed could happen to a man when he'd been caught red-handed in the meat section using the big roll of oversize plastic wrap to sheathe a naked cashier. Don had insisted it was groundbreaking performance art. Alice had insisted it was grounds for performing a divorce.

Yeah, small-town life really wasn't what Sam had expected at all.

"Alice!" he heard Don yell again on the other side of the mirror. The man sounded nervous and more than a little agitated. "I've got something for you! You've been asking for it! You deserve it! And now you're gonna get it! But good!"

And with that, Don did indeed begin to wave something around. When Sam saw what it was, a cold, unpleasant sensation slithered into his belly. Because what Don was holding was a helluva lot more menacing than a not-on-sale Juiceman. And it could go off any minute. Worst of all, however, Don was standing right next to Rosie Bliss.

ROSIE WAS BATTLING a bizarre sensation of being watched when Alice's husband, Don, came barreling into the aerobics studio out of nowhere. Again. As usual, he looked out of breath and anxious, and Rosie hoped he didn't drop onto his knees and plead with Alice to take him back, the way he had last week when he'd barreled into the aerobics studio out of nowhere. Because it had taken all six class members to help him stand up again, so bad were his knees. Not so usual, though, this time Don was brandishing a… Brandishing a…a…a…

What the hell? Rosie thought when she recognized the thing in Don's hand. It looked like…

Nah, she immediately assured herself. It couldn't be. Not a nice old guy like Don. He might be a little off these days, what with shrouding cashiers in Glad Wrap and threatening to throw Alice into financial turmoil with frivolous shopping, but he wasn't the sort of man to go out in public with a…with a…a…a…

A vibrator?

Rosie tilted her head to the side, to observe the object from another angle. Yep, Don was brandishing a vibrator all right. The Xtacy 3000 model, if she wasn't mistaken. In the Vixen Scarlet color that was so hard to find these days. Even on the Internet. Rosie was fairly familiar with the product, since she'd been shopping around for one for the past month herself, wanting to upgrade from her Xtacy 2000.

Well, what else was she supposed to do? Small-town life agreed with her in a lot of ways—ways she hadn't even anticipated, truth be told—but Northaven wasn't exactly bursting at the seams with eligible men. At least those under the age of seventy-five. Even if ol' Don was estranged from Alice now, it would take a lot more than an Xtacy 3000 in Vixen Scarlet to make Rosie think twice about dating him. Which was moot, anyway, since he was clearly still deeply in love with his wife, performance art with his head cashier notwithstanding.

Of course, there *was* Northaven's incredibly hunky police chief, Rosie thought. As she often did. Especially when she was keeping company with her Xtacy 2000. Not only was he way younger than seventy-five—she guesstimated he was in his mid- to late-thirties—but with that thick dark hair and those chocolate-brown eyes…and those broad shoulders that strained at the seams of his white cop shirt in the warmer months and his leather cop jacket in the winter…and that perfectly packaged rump that even brown twill cop pants couldn't mar…and those big manly hands, each of which would *very* nicely cover a woman's breast or splay lovingly over a woman's behind….

Damn. As always, she was getting way ahead of herself when there was no way she'd be getting any. Not from Sam Maguire, at any rate. Because he evidently didn't notice the steamy heat ballooning around the two of them that Rosie noticed whenever they encountered each other. Possibly because the steamy heat was only ballooning off of her. Even though she always made a point to seek Sam out on those occasions when they were attending the same function, he only greeted her politely, made a little small talk, then found some reason why he had to go speak to someone else before politely excusing himself to do just that.

The first couple of times it had happened, Rosie hadn't thought much about it. He was a public servant, after all, and new in town to boot, so he'd naturally need to make himself available to a lot of people. She'd finally taken the hint, though, the last time she'd encountered him at a Chamber of Commerce gathering, when Sam had excused himself to have a very important discussion with Luther Bybee. No one in Northaven ever *elected* to have a discussion with Luther Bybee. Because Luther Bybee was notorious in Northaven for repeating the same story over and over again about the genital wart that nearly claimed his life. Clearly Sam wasn't interested in Rosie romantically. Fortunately, her Xtacy 2000 was always there when she needed it.

She knew Alice had been looking for the new Xtacy 3000, too—Hey, what woman wasn't?—and thought it was exceedingly nice of Don to have found one for her. It took a special man to extend a vibrating olive branch. Maybe he really was into nude, plastic wrap performance art. Stranger things had happened. Don was obviously doing his best to make amends for the cashier thing.

Rosie was taking a step forward to get a better look at the vibrator and was about to ask Don where he'd found it, especially in the most sought-after color, but her words—and her step, for that matter—were cut short when, out of nowhere, she was blindsided by a huge, growling grizzly bear that wrestled her to the floor and rolled on top of her.

Oh, no, wait. It wasn't a grizzly bear, she realized when she and the big predator came to a halt. It was Sam Maguire. Speak of the devilishly handsome. Maybe he *was* interested in her romantically. Though why he'd decided to make his intentions known so suddenly, in such a public venue was a little puzzling. And just where the hell had he come from, anyway? He wasn't enrolled in Alice's morning class.

"Uh, Chief?" she said by way of a greeting.

But she got lost after that, because she couldn't seem to find her way out of those espresso eyes and back to…whatever she'd been doing before she found herself pinned beneath him. All she could remember was something about nudity and plastic wrap and performing, all of which sounded pretty good at the moment.

He was solid rock in all the places he came into contact with her, shoulder to shoulder, chest to calf, his rigid weight pinning her to the padded mat beneath her in a way that should probably have been painful, considering his size, but which was instead incredibly erotic—considering his size. She wasn't positive, but Rosie was pretty sure that *wasn't* a banana in his pocket. He was definitely happy to see her. Really happy, judging by the size of that banana. Colossally happy. In fact, it wasn't so much a banana he had in his pocket as it was a loaf of French bread.

He smelled wonderful, an enticing mix of clean laundry and autumn wind. And something else, too, something intangible and implacable that was earthy and musky and dark. Something so intrinsically male that Rosie began to wonder how she could ever think an Xtacy 2000—or even an Xtacy 3000—could ever be enough.

And those dark, fathomless brown eyes of his… She'd always thought Sam's eyes reflected intelligence and good humor, but up close this way, she saw that both were tempered by something less noble and more unpredictable…and held just barely at bay. The impression never quite had the chance to gel in her brain—not that much could gel in her brain with Sam Maguire lying atop her this way—because he rolled again, this time pulling Rosie on top of himself, a position she immediately decided she liked even better. Unfortunately, that impression, too, was quickly dispelled when Sam effortlessly picked her up and set her down on the mat beside him.

Truly. He picked her up as easily as if she had been a ladybug who landed on his shirt, then set her down with a gentleness she wouldn't have thought he was capable of managing. And, just like that, he went from being sexy as hell to flat-out irresistible.

"Uh, sorry," he said by way of an apology.

For one much-too-brief moment, their eyes met again, and he studied her face as if she were the answer to every frustrated question and desperate plea he'd ever shot at the cosmos. And in that much-too-brief moment, Rosie felt like a blessing indeed. Then he was scrambling up off the floor and straightening, and the feeling evaporated like, inescapably, ballooning steam. Where Rosie had expected him to extend a hand to help her up, however, he grabbed Don instead, circling one big hand around the man's wrist to twist his arm behind his back before snaking the other out to grab the Xtacy 3000 from Don's grip.

Wow. Sam must want one of those even more than Rosie did.

She shook the thought from her head as soon as it formed, since any man who carried around a loaf of French bread in his pocket certainly didn't need a little thing like an Xtacy vibrator. Funny, though, how she'd never considered the Xtacy little before....

"Chief Maguire!" Alice shouted when she saw Sam manhandling her husband.

She dropped her hands to her pink-leotard-clad hips and blew a damp, silvery blond curl off her forehead, only to have it fall right back into place. Alice was really too petite and willowy to look menacing, Rosie thought, but damned if she didn't come pretty close just then.

"What do you think you're doing to Donnie?" Alice demanded.

Donnie? Rosie echoed to herself. Alice only called Don "Donnie" when she was speaking affectionately about him. In fact, she hadn't even called him "Don" lately. Since the plastic-wrapped cashier episode a few weeks ago, she'd been referring to him as—

Well, something that wasn't fit to share in any company, mixed or otherwise. Suffice it to say it had been a *looooong* time since Rosie had heard Alice refer to her husband in anything remotely resembling affectionate terms. In fact, what she'd called him had been pretty much anatomically impossible anyway, even if one had a loaf of French bread in one's pocket to do it with. Now, however, it looked like Alice was reconsidering her animosity. Among other things. Because she walked right up to Sam and stomped on his toe. Hard.

"Ow," Sam replied with much understatement. He lifted the injured foot from the floor, but didn't loosen his hold on Don. "What was that for?"

"You leave my Donnie alone," Alice told him, hands fisted indignantly on her hips again.

"Leave him alone?" Sam echoed. "You asked me to intervene if he tried anything funny. So I'm intervening." He rubbed his foot on the back of his calf and put it—gingerly—on the floor again. "And you're this close to assaulting an officer, Alice."

Alice snorted derisively. "Oh, please. I barely touched you."

Rosie would bet a fallen arch that Sam disagreed. To his credit, however, he said nothing.

"Now let Donnie go," Alice repeated. "He's brought me a present."

With obvious reluctance, Sam did as Alice asked, but he didn't fork over the vibrator, only looked at it curiously, as if he had no idea what it was. Then, "I have no idea what this is," he said. "I came running in because when I first saw it, I thought it was a stick of dynamite."

Rosie couldn't quite help the smile that curled her lips. "Well, it can be," she said. "In the right hands."

The other women in the class chuckled knowingly, something that clearly only confused Sam more. Alice, however, saved Rosie from having to explain by snatching the vibrator out of Sam's hand and turning it on. It immediately relaxed from its erect cylindrical shape and began to twist itself into a series of elaborate, contorted motions that Rosie knew could be set at a variety of speeds, intensities and temperatures. It was erotic poetry in motion.

"It's the Xtacy 3000," Alice said for Sam's enlightenment. "A personal fulfillment device."

"Personal fulfillment device," Sam said without any enlightenment whatsoever.

Then again, he was obviously the kind of man who could personally fulfill a woman to the point where she wouldn't need a device for that, so Rosie supposed it shouldn't be surprising that he'd have no knowledge of such things.

Alice rolled her eyes and blew out an exasperated sigh. "A vibrator," she clarified.

Sam's dark brows shot up at that, and a faint stain of pink bloomed on his cheeks. Oh, for God's sake, Rosie

thought. He was blushing. Honestly *blushing*. She didn't
think she'd ever seen such a manly man do something
so adorable. That Sam was doing it only made him so
much sexier. And so much more irresistible.

"I had it on my Christmas list last year," Alice continued as she watched the vibrator do its thing. "But
the demand has been so high since it hit the market that
it's been impossible to find. Especially in this color."
Her voice softening, she looked at her husband and
added, "Oh, Donnie. You do still love me. Wherever
did you find it?"

And with that, she tucked herself under Don's now-
freed arm and snuggled against him with such obvious,
unmitigated love that Rosie couldn't help but smile.
Wow. Someday, she hoped she'd find a guy like Don.
Only without the comb-over and the green Clover Mart
jacket. One who would understand her needs and
desires and do his best to fulfill them while loving her
to distraction.

Inevitably, her gaze wandered to Sam, and she saw
that he was watching the Xtacy 3000 intently. But he
didn't look in any way turned-on, the way the women
in the group did, Rosie couldn't help thinking. Instead,
he was looking at it as if he were wondering what kind
of addition it would be to his Craftsman tool collection.

Men. They just couldn't see the erotic side of machin-
ery. She wondered what he'd say if she told him how
many women had discovered dual uses for everything
from hand mixers to washing machines. Or was it just
Rosie who had discovered dual uses for stuff like that…?

Sam watched warily for a moment as Alice and Don

continued to snuggle, then his expression softened. Well, okay, maybe *softened* was a little too extreme a word to use, since what his expression actually did was…um…become less hard. Then he lifted a hand to the back of his neck and rubbed it in that way men did when they were a little uncomfortable about something.

He asked, "So, Alice, does this mean you won't need me to include your house and studio on my daily rounds anymore?"

For a minute, Rosie didn't think Alice had heard the question, but then she turned a distracted gaze to Sam, as if she only now remembered where she was and what was going on. She seemed to remember then, too, how she'd been mad at Don for weeks, because she pushed herself away from him and fisted her hands on her hips again, making a halfhearted attempt to look angry.

But the resentment in her voice was clearly forced when she said, "Well, Don and I have a lot to talk about. Just because he brought me a gift doesn't mean all is forgiven."

Hah, Rosie thought with a smile. That wasn't just any gift.

"But no, Chief," Alice told him, "you don't have to stop by anymore. For now," she added with a chilly look at Don…which inevitably turned into a warm smile.

Sam dropped his hand back to his side and nodded, then turned to go. He first strode past the line of women, including Rosie, without looking at any of them. But as he gripped the handle of the studio door, he pivoted back around and met her gaze levelly with his own. "I'm sorry about sacking you the way I did," he told her.

Well, that made one of them, Rosie thought.

"I was aiming for Don," he added. "Then you stepped in front of him, and…" His voice trailed off, since it really wasn't necessary to say anything more.

She started to tell him it was okay, that his sacking her had in fact been the closest thing she'd had to a sexual encounter with a living, breathing man in a long time, and could they possibly get together for another sacking sometime soon? But she checked herself after a simple, "That's okay."

He started to turn around again, but halted, clearly wanting to say something he wasn't sure how to say. Finally, though, his gaze ricocheting now from Rosie's face to the wall behind her, he asked, "How do you know it can be a stick of dynamite in the right hands?"

In lieu of a response, Rosie waited until he was looking at her again, then she lifted both hands and wiggled her fingers at him.

He arched his brows again, and she watched to see if he would blush as he had before. He didn't. But his dark eyes grew darker, and his lips parted fractionally, as if he suddenly needed more air. He didn't say anything else after that, only spun around again and made his way out of the studio. Rosie's gaze fell to his rump as he went, then climbed to those broad shoulders straining at the seams of his white cop shirt. She remembered how happy he'd been to see her when he was lying on top of her.

And, just like that, all thoughts of the Xtacy 3000 were gone.

2

ONE THING ABOUT small-town Northaven that hadn't surprised Sam was its police station. Nestled at the center of Main Street in what was called the town's historic quarter, it was housed in a restored brick-front building that hosted several small businesses—one of which just happened to be Rosie Bliss's flower shop, Kabloom, three doors down. The walkway outside was cobbled, of course; the windows were paned, naturally; and the interior could only be described as quaint, a word Sam normally, manfully, avoided.

But there was no other term to capture the mood of the hardwood floors and plaster walls painted what Vicky, their dispatcher, called Wedgwood blue. Whatever the hell that was. The desks—all three of them—were antique monstrosities that could comfortably serve dinner for twelve, and the chairs were spindled wooden numbers that creaked comfortably whenever anyone sat down. In fact, the creaking of chairs and floors made up the bulk of the sounds in the place, interrupted only by the soft strains of music from the radio, which Vicky kept tuned to a light jazz station.

It was nothing like the soulless cinder block and

dented metal and cracked plastic of Sam's Boston precinct. And the stench of too many unwashed perps and overworked cops had been replaced by freshly baked bread from Barb's Bohemian Bakery next door. Also absent was the constant ringing of phones, the whining and jeering of the hookers and pushers in the cages, and the free-flowing profanity of his colleagues. Sam, like his two full-time deputies and the half-dozen volunteer deputies who visited the precinct from time to time, had learned to watch his language, because Vicky fined anyone who swore within her hearing a dollar for every inappropriate word used. Then she donated the money to the Northaven Free Public Library.

The new Maguire Browsing Collection was named after Sam, since the bulk of his first year's paychecks had gone to Vicky.

As different as his life in Northaven was, however, he wouldn't go back to Boston for a million bucks. He might never quite get used to living here, but he liked it. A lot. It appealed to that thing inside him that had made him become a cop to begin with—a belief that decency and goodness did exist in the world. In Boston, he'd begun to think that was only a fantasy. But it was true in places like Northaven, places that needed to be protected at all costs. So Sam would do his best to keep the small town and all its residents safe from outside corruption. Of course, now that he knew women like Alice Stuckey and Rosie Bliss—and the handful of other women in the morning aerobics class—were all vibrator enthusiasts….

He gave his head a hard shake as he pushed open the

door to the precinct, in the hopes that doing so would chase away the image of Rosie, buck naked and flat on her back, legs spread wide and hips thrusting upward as she did things to herself with that vibrator he'd much rather be doing to her himself.

He bit back a groan as he strode into the precinct, hoping Vicky didn't notice he had a woody at half-mast. But she had her dark blond head bent over a book, as she usually did during non-crime-spree times—which was pretty much always. To add a bit of color to her dispatcher's uniform of white shirt and brown pants, she regularly added a sweater in a different color. Today's was red. It matched the scrap of fabric she'd used to pull her curly hair back into a stubby ponytail.

"Any calls?" Sam asked as he hurried past her desk, trying to keep his back to her and his woody to himself.

"Only one for you specifically," she told him. She turned in her chair to look at him as he seated himself at his desk. "From Ed Dinwiddie at campus security. Again."

"The usual?" Sam asked.

"The usual," Vicky confirmed. "He's still sure there's someone selling drugs at Northaven College, and he wants to coordinate with you on an investigation and possible stakeout."

Sam didn't bother to hide his groan this time, since it was one of regular frustration, and not the sexual kind. Ed Dinwiddie, the chief of security at Northaven College, had been sure someone was peddling drugs on campus since before Sam's arrival in town. At first, Sam had taken the other man's suspicions seriously, because he hadn't had any reason not to. But a brief investigation had produced nothing but Ed's overactive imagination to support the existence of anything narcotic going on at Northaven—save a lot of caffeine abuse and OD'ing on Green Day around midterm and finals time. Then, when Bruno and Dalton, Sam's two full-time deputies, had assured Sam there was nothing out of the ordinary going on because they'd investigated it themselves a time or two, Sam had let the matter drop.

Ed, however, hadn't.

He sent monthly reports to Sam describing in detail his suspicions and everything that made him suspicious. The problem was that Ed Dinwiddie found suspicious anything from what he considered incriminating dialogue between students—which consisted largely of slang words for coffee and oral sex—to what he was sure was drug paraphernalia—even though the last bit of "paraphernalia" Ed had found turned out to be a popcorn popper. He also made regular monthly calls to Sam to "coordinate" an investigation. Sam had tried to be polite, but he'd never been known for his patience, and what little he had was beginning to wear thin.

"Does Ed have any additional evidence this time to support his suspicions?" Sam asked Vicky wearily, already sure of the answer.

"It's more paraphernalia this month," she said. "Though what he described to me sounds a lot like the rhinestone- and stud-setter I got for my twelfth birthday thirty years ago."

Sam grunted in resignation. "Yeah, I hear those things are making a comeback."

"There was one thing Ed had this time, though, that

was a little out of the ordinary," Vicky added, voicing the revelation with clear glee. Her green eyes fairly sparkled with mischief. "Something he's for sure never mentioned having before."

"What's that?" Sam asked with much disinterest, reaching for the small stack of mail perched near the edge of his desk.

"Well, I don't know where or how he came by the information," Vicky said, "but this time, Ed told me he's got himself a bona fide suspect who he's absolutely positive is selling drugs to the Northaven students." When Sam glanced up, she smiled and wiggled her eyebrows in way that was far more playful than it was concerned. "And, Sam, this time, Ed even gave me a name."

"ROSIE, YOU HAVE TO help me. You have what he needs. And if he doesn't get it soon, he's going to *die.* And if he dies, *I'll* die. I need for him to be at his best. And he can't be at his best without it."

Behind the counter of her flower shop, Rosie rolled her eyes at the young woman and sighed. College girls. Such drama. Such pathos. Everybody was always going to *die* over something. Shannon Eckert was no different. The dark-haired, dark-eyed beauty on the other side of the counter was relentlessly thin, her cropped purple sweater riding high above her low-slung blue jeans to reveal a dangling rhinestone palm tree that winked from her navel. Her hair was tucked behind ears that boasted another half-dozen piercings, and a wreath of roses was tattooed around one wrist.

Rosie's own appearance paled by comparison—and

not just because of her fairer features, either. The only body parts that were pierced on her own person these days were her eardrums—thanks in large part to Shannon's shrieking just now—and she'd had the circled A tattoo above her ankle—the symbol for anarchy—surgically buffed away years ago. Her attire consisted of a crinkly emerald skirt shot through with threads of silver, and a loose-fitting white tunic she'd cinched with a macramé belt.

Had someone told her fifteen years ago that she would be dressing like a gypsy and selling flowers for a living, Rosie would have laughed in that person's face. Back then, she'd worn all black, all the time, right down to the heavy kohl around her eyes and the polish on her fingernails. She'd even dyed her hair black. In fact, it wasn't until she'd gone back to her natural color a few years ago that she'd realized she'd gone from the carrot orange of her childhood to a more sophisticated dark auburn.

She'd been one crazy, mixed-up kid when she was a teenager, no two ways about it. Mixed-up to a point that had earned her more trouble than any teenager deserved—or could handle. She'd come a long way since South Beach. And she never, ever, wanted to go back. Not even if it wouldn't put her life in danger to do so.

"I'm serious," Shannon continued, tugging Rosie back to the present, where she would much rather be. "He's getting shaky, he's gone so long without it."

"Mmm-hmm," Rosie said without concern. Somehow, she suspected Shannon was actually the shaky one. "And just how long has it been, Shannon? A day? Two?"

"Three!" the girl fairly screamed. "It's been three

days! You've got to help! You've got to give me more of that stuff!"

Rosie shook her head. "Three days, huh? Wow. Must be hell."

"It *is!*" Shannon cried.

"Fine," Rosie said, finally capitulating.

She went to the back of her shop and opened the cabinet where she kept her special orders. From the middle shelf, she withdrew an oversize basket that held an assortment of small fabric pouches. Each was filled with a substance that had become extremely popular among the upper classmen at little Northaven College, to the point where they had even developed a slang name for it—Rapture. Many even swore they were hooked on it for life. To Rosie, such monikers and claims were a little over-the-top. What the pouches held was simply a sideline to her business, one she was keeping under wraps for two reasons.

Number one, she honestly wasn't sure what the reaction and reception to her products would be outside her clientele list. Aphrodisiacs weren't exactly a commonplace commercial product, and anything that was even remotely sexual in nature was often viewed in a less than positive light. At best, her products might be snickered at if Rosie advertised them, and at worst, they might fall under suspicion. The citizens of Northaven— at least the ones who purchased her special orders— were surprisingly open-minded about the herbal aphrodisiac teas she blended for them. But it was still a small town in New England, with its Puritan sensibilities, and Rosie preferred to err on the side of caution.

Her second reason for not advertising her aphrodisiac teas was the same reason she didn't much advertise the floral side of her business. Maintaining a low profile was essential to Rosie's well-being. Hell, it was essential to her very life. Her aphrodisiacs were very effective, and they were the sort of thing that might even potentially achieve cult status popularity among the university or online crowd. Worst-case scenario, it was possible she could see some press for them. Even locally, that could be disastrous. The last thing she needed or wanted was to draw attention to herself. When she'd been in the spotlight before, she'd nearly ended up dead. So, like everything else in her world, Rosie kept the aphrodisiacs under wraps and relied on referrals and word of mouth to promote them.

So far, so good.

Now she fished a pouch bearing Shannon's name out of the basket before replacing the rest of the assortment in the cabinet. Then she returned to the front of the store where her client stood fairly humming with anticipation. Rosie extended the fabric bag toward the young woman, who immediately made a grab for it. But she snatched it back before Shannon could claim it.

"Go easy on this stuff," she cautioned the girl. "There's more to college than partying, you know. You need to get an education in there somewhere."

Shannon nodded impatiently. "It's not for me," she told Rosie. "It's for Devin."

"Sure it is," Rosie said. She'd heard that one before. All the girls *said* they were buying it for their boyfriends, that the guys were the ones who really needed it. But Rosie knew the women enjoyed the results just as much as their menfolk—probably more.

Shannon dug into her pocket for a rumpled bill and handed it to Rosie, who then reluctantly handed over the pouch. "I mean it, Shannon," she said as she released it. "I know classes just started up again a month ago, but you need to focus on your studies, not Devin."

Shannon nodded again, more slowly this time, seeming to feel a little calmer now that she had what she'd come for. "I know," she said. "I'm totally focused on my studies, honest. But Devin is so fine, and I want to be with him. I want him to be happy. And I want to be happy, too." She smiled and leaned in a little, lowering her voice some as she added, "We're getting married next summer after graduation, did I tell you?"

Rosie smiled back. "No, you didn't," she said, genuinely delighted to hear the news. "Congratulations. That's great. How long have you two been together?"

"Since high school," Shannon told her, sounding almost bashful now. She held up the fabric pouch Rosie had just handed her. "Maybe you can give me a lifetime supply of this for my wedding present, huh?"

Rosie shook her head. "Not a chance. You won't need that once you're married."

Shannon expelled a dubious sound. "Are you kidding? That's when I'll need it the most."

Rosie shook her head again. "I'm sure it's just the pressures of college that are making Devin…you know."

Shannon made a wistful sound now. "I hope you're right," she said. She fiddled with the pouch again. "I guess it would be pretty bad to have to rely on this stuff for the rest of our lives, wouldn't it?"

"You won't need it," Rosie assured her. "You guys will be fine."

Shannon eyed her thoughtfully for a moment. "As long as you're here for now," she said, "supplying us with what we need. Thanks, Rosie." And with that, she spun on her heel and left the store.

Kids, Rosie thought, ignoring the fact that there was barely a decade between her and Shannon's age. Some people grew up a lot faster than others. And Rosie should know. She hadn't been a kid since… Well. She hadn't even been a kid when she *was* a kid.

Before more thoughts of the past could put her into a less-than-cheerful mood, she pushed them to the very back of her brain, where she relegated all the things that threatened to stain the picture-perfect life she was trying to paint for herself in Northaven. She'd struggled through a lot to get where she was, dammit. She was a survivor in the strictest sense of the word. She'd worked hard to achieve a fragile kind of satisfaction—with her life and herself—that she wouldn't mess with for anything. And she was still working hard, still trying to move forward. Even if Kabloom wasn't a booming success, she was still turning a profit at the end of every month.

Okay, so maybe she hadn't shown the best judgment, opening a florist and organic gardening shop in a town that catered to young, carefree students who didn't give a second—or even first—thought to such things. But there were only a handful of florists in the entire county—

and none in Northaven proper—so when someone did need flowers, they called Kabloom to order them.

Besides, her aphrodisiac business *had* begun to flourish over the past six months, even though she hadn't gone out of her way to advertise it. And that *was* a direct result of living in a college town. Rosie hadn't consciously considered the benefits of that, but the college atmosphere here did foster a culture of more tolerance—and even enthusiasm—about her products. She was grateful to the campus crowd for taking such an interest. Word of mouth alone had been phenomenal.

It had even traveled beyond campus. She had clients now who were scions of the community. You really couldn't judge a book by its cover. Or even the mayor of Northaven, since she was one of Rosie's biggest customers.

Rosie sighed as she looked around her shop. Her *empty* shop. Her empty shop that was empty most of the time—save those busy lunchtimes when so many Northaven students came in to pick up their special orders. Rosie hadn't even had to hire another employee, since she kept only daytime hours. Save a handful of feminine holidays like Valentine's Day and Mother's Day, any traffic she saw in the shop was sporadic. When she'd come to Northaven two years ago after everything went to hell in Boulder, she'd had hopes for building her business a little faster, but at this rate… Well, thank goodness people here died on a regular basis, so at least she had the funeral orders.

And that, more than anything, told Rosie she couldn't afford to skimp on the aphrodisiac side of the business.

Because, call her crazy, being grateful for the death of one's neighbors did *not* seem like a sound business plan. In fact, it seemed kinda ooky.

Her gaze strayed to the back of the shop and fell on the cabinet from which she had just pulled Shannon's special order. Maybe, if she was very, very careful, she could expand a little bit on her aphrodisiacs. Start looking into other preparations that might have the same effect as the teas she blended for her customers. Incense, maybe. Massage oils. Candies. As long as Rosie stayed behind the scenes herself and never became a public persona, she shouldn't have any problems. That had been what caused the trouble in Boulder. Putting a public face onto her work.

Yeah, maybe she should start focusing a little more of her professional efforts where they would turn the greatest profit, even if that profitable area wasn't exactly—to some people's way of thinking anyway—conventional. There had been a time in the nation's history, after all, when a respectable woman couldn't even buy a cocktail legally. These days, you'd be hard pressed to find a social gathering where someone *wasn't* drinking. A few years from now, what Rosie was selling from that cabinet might very well be the centerpiece at every party. Why shouldn't she be the front-runner as a supplier?

Hey, who was there in Northaven to say she couldn't?

SAM CURBED HIS IMPULSE to flee as he folded himself into the chair before Ed Dinwiddie's desk at the Northaven College Campus Security Office. Although the college could have been the poster child for New England

Liberal Arts schools right down to its pillared entrances and ivy-encrusted brick walls, the decor of campus security was nowhere close to the quaintness of the Northaven police station. In fact, Ed's office had a lot in common with Sam's Boston precinct, and somehow Sam got the feeling it was because Ed wanted it that way to make himself feel more like a real, live cop.

His desk was a scarred, ugly gray metal thing, his chair a beat-up number upholstered with cheap soiled fabric and wheels that cried out in pain when Ed settled his ample frame into it. The only decorations on the grayish-white walls were framed awards of dubious origin with Ed's name emblazoned on them, and a handful of eight-by-tens of Ed shaking hands with people, most of whom Sam recognized as members of the Northaven Chamber of Commerce. It was all Ed, all the time, and it was more than a little creepy.

"Vicky tells me you have a suspect in the campus narcotics traffic," Sam said to open the conversation, wanting to get this over with as quickly as possible. He didn't bother to point out that there was no actual proof of any campus narcotics traffic. Ed would have just taken ten minutes to insist otherwise.

"I do," Ed told him. "Rosie Bliss."

Wow. Sam hadn't thought it could sound any more ridiculous a second time, but coming from Ed's mouth, the suggestion that Rosie was peddling dope sounded even sillier than when Vicky had said it. And Vicky had been laughing hysterically at the time.

"Rosie Bliss," Sam echoed, swallowing the hysterical laughter he felt threatening himself.

"Yep," Ed said with complete confidence, running a hand over his graying crew cut.

Sam inhaled a deep breath and released it slowly. Only when he was certain he could continue with a straight face did he do so. "And what leads you to this conclusion, Ed?"

"Well, it makes perfect sense, doesn't it?" the other man countered. "The drug traffic on campus started not long after she moved here. She owns a flower shop, for God's sake, so she must know all about plants and how to grow them illicitly. Kids go into her shop on a regular basis but rarely come out with flowers or plants. At least none that I can see."

Sam eyed the other man levelly, not much liking what he was hearing. "Are you telling me you've been staking out Rosie's shop?"

"Not at all," Ed assured him in a way that was in no way reassuring. "I eat lunch in the square when the weather's nice, and I've just happened to notice that lunch hour is often a pretty busy time for Kabloom. Only the kids that go in there don't seem to be coming out with anything."

"Maybe they're ordering flowers to be delivered," Sam suggested.

"Maybe," Ed conceded. "But I doubt it."

"Maybe Rosie's just popular with the college crowd," Sam further posited. "She's not that much older than they are. Maybe she's just made a lot of friends since moving to town."

"Oh, she's popular, all right," Ed agreed readily. "And she's made *lots* of friends. Because she's supplying them with drugs."

Sam uncrossed his legs and leaned forward, propping his elbows on his knees. This really had to stop. If Sam didn't dissuade Ed from his belief in Rosie's guilt, he could potentially start skirting harassment behavior. Maybe even stalking behavior. Ed did seem to have one of those borderline personalities. Of course, Sam thought further, just about everyone in Northaven was at least a little surreal.

"Look, Ed," he began, "I appreciate all the hours you've put in on this thing, but—"

Ed started talking again before Sam had a chance to finish. "And then there's the fact that no record of Rosie Bliss exists anywhere in the entire United States."

Okay, that got Sam's attention. Not so much the part about there being no evidence of Rosie Bliss's existence, but that Ed had taken it upon himself to look into Rosie's background and had possibly violated police procedure— not to mention Rosie's basic human rights—to do it.

"Ed, seeing as how you're head of *campus* security," Sam said cautiously, "I'm not sure it's within your jurisdiction to run a background check on a Northaven citizen."

Ed seemed in no way perturbed by Sam's suggestion that he may have overstepped the bounds of his position. On the contrary, looking quite calm and complacent, he turned around to face his computer, typed a few keys and then moved out of the way. "Switchboard-dot-com," he said as his browser opened a page on the Internet. "It's a matter of public record for any *private citizen* who might be interested in looking."

Sam duly noted the other man's emphasis on the phrase that indicated he hadn't been snooping on Rosie's private life while he was on the clock. Which, it went without saying, was a *huge* reassurance to Sam. Not.

"No Rosie Blisses are listed in the entire United States," Ed continued. "Not even in Northaven."

"Ed," Sam said patiently, "Switchboard-dot-com is an online phone directory. If someone has an unlisted number, it won't show up there. Obviously, Rosie's kept her number unlisted, which is something a lot of women who live alone choose to do for the sake of security."

Ed blinked at him, looking a little nonplussed now. But all he said in reply was, "Oh."

"Besides, Rosie's probably a nickname," Sam pointed out. "Try Rose Bliss this time." And he tried not to think about how he was just encouraging Ed. Okay, so maybe he was interested in Rosie, too. Just in a non-criminal way. Except for the fact that the way she made him feel sexually was actually pretty criminal.

Ed turned back to the computer and entered the altered information, and this time more than a dozen names appeared.

"See there?" Sam said.

"There's not one listed for Northaven," Ed pointed out, though with considerably less flair this time.

"Like I said, Ed. Unlisted."

Sam thought the other man would just let it go at that, and started to rise to make his way out. But he halted when Ed reached for the gold-tone badge pinned to his blue uniform shirt and unpinned it, then unhitched the gun on his belt and set it on the desk.

"Oh, now, Ed, there's no reason to go to that extreme," Sam hastily reassured him, taking his seat once more. "You don't have to resign over something like this. It's no big deal, really. You and I can just keep your investigation of Rosie Bliss that may or may not be a violation of police procedure," he inserted meaningfully, since it never hurt to emphasize a reminder like that, "between ourselves. No one else has to know. Now put your badge and gun back where they belong."

Ed looked confused for a minute, then when he seemed to understand what Sam had said he looked shocked. "Resign?" he echoed indignantly. "I'm not resigning. I'm taking a break. As of this moment, I'm a private citizen, off the clock." He pointed to his watch. "It's lunch hour. Man's gotta eat." And with that, he pulled a paper sack out of the side desk drawer and unwrapped a sandwich, chips and can of soda.

Feeling a little confused himself now, Sam nevertheless said, "Well, then, I'll be off." Though he still wasn't confident Ed had let the matter of Rosie Bliss go.

That was only reinforced when Ed said, "And maybe while I'm having lunch, I'll just do a little surfing on the 'Net. I like to surf the 'Net to search for things. Search for people. You never know what'll turn up. You ever surf the 'Net, Sam?"

Sam closed his eyes and counted slowly to ten. However, it was less because he was trying to manage his impatience with Ed and more because he was trying not to think about, ah, *surfing the 'Net* of someone whose net he very much wanted to, ah, *surf*. In fact, he was probably thinking about, ah, *surfing* the net of the same person Ed wanted to surf the 'Net for. Just, you know, not in any Internet sense of the word.

"Ed…" he began wearily.

But Ed had turned around to the computer again, and was punching more keys. This time, the Web site that popped up on the screen was for an online private investigative firm called WeFindEm.com. In big red letters at the top, it said, When You Can't Find 'Em, We Can! And We Can Find Out Things About 'Em You Never Knew! In A Matter Of Minutes! In smaller letters, it said how much it would cost someone to have We-FindEm.com do just that. Very little, to Sam's way of thinking. Amazing how people's lives and secrets could be purchased so reasonably on the Internet.

"So since I'm on my lunch hour," Ed said, "and since I'm not, technically, in uniform, I'm visiting this site as a private citizen. Which means I'm not violating police procedure."

Maybe, Sam thought. It was a blurry line Ed was walking. Of course, it really didn't matter, since the idea of Rosie Bliss being a drug pusher was still laughable, so any information Ed may uncover about her—or even purchase about her—was beside the point. If it was even reliable. Were those online investigators monitored? Hell, were they even licensed? Who knew what Ed would get for his $49.99? Other than the shaft? $99.99 if he wanted Rosie's criminal records along with the shaft.

"Ed," Sam began again.

He chose his words carefully, reminded himself to be gentle. It was common knowledge in Northaven that Ed Dinwiddie's dream in life was to make a major bust that would gain him national acclaim. It was also common knowledge in Northaven that that wasn't likely as long as he was head of security at the college. Hell, Ed being Ed, that wasn't likely to happen even if he found a job with a metropolitan police department. Any force in their right minds—assuming they lost their minds long enough to hire Ed in the first place—would assign him to desk duty. Preferably in the fund-raising department where the most damage he could do would be to the decorating committee of the Policeman's Ball.

"This'll just take a few minutes," Ed said as he turned to the computer, pulling his wallet out of his back pocket as he did.

"Ed," Sam tried again.

But Ed started humming "Stairway to Heaven"— loudly—interspersing it with admonitions like, "I can't hear you. I'm humming 'Stairway to Heaven.' La la la la la. I can't hear you. Buy-ing…the stair-way…to heaven. La la la."

So Sam had no choice but to give up and accept the inevitable. The inevitable being that Ed wasn't going to let this go until Sam had had a look at the report with him. Which actually might not be such a bad thing. Because once that report came through and showed that Rosie Bliss wasn't the hardened criminal Ed was certain she was, he'd have no choice but to abandon his conviction and leave Rosie alone.

WeFindEm.com was as good as their word, and by the time Ed finished his lunch—and a few more fractured Led Zeppelin numbers—the computer was telling him he had mail. The report was attached, and Ed immediately printed up two copies, one for himself, and one for Sam, who accepted it grudgingly and gave it a perfunctory look.

The look became less perfunctory, however, as the information became more inculpatory. Because if We-FindEm.com was right, Rosie Bliss *hadn't* existed anywhere in the entire United States before she moved to Northaven.

"There you go," Ed said triumphantly, having obviously read to the end as Sam had. "No evidence of Rosie Bliss's existence prior to her having moved here two years ago. No birth records, no work records, no addresses, no licenses for anything, nothing. She doesn't show up anywhere until she moved here." He glanced up at Sam, looking even more triumphant than he sounded. "Now how do you think she's made her way as an adult without having a bank account, owning property or applying for a job? The first time her name shows up as having any of those things, it's here in Northaven." He pointed to the investigative report before adding, "And look at this. She doesn't even have a mortgage on Kabloom. When she bought it two years ago, she paid for it in full, to the tune of a hundred and fifty-eight thousand dollars. Cash."

"That doesn't make her a criminal, Ed," Sam pointed out. But even he was starting to feel a little niggle of suspicion at the back of his brain. What Ed had discovered about Rosie *was* a little odd.

"Maybe not," the other man conceded with clear reluctance. He pointed to the investigative report. "But this sure isn't the report of a person who has nothing to hide."

"Maybe she's an heiress," Sam said. Not that he believed it for a minute. The last thing Rosie acted or seemed like was a person from a monied, privileged background. "She never had to work or live anywhere other than with Mommy and Daddy Warbucks, who took care of everything for her."

"That still doesn't explain why she doesn't have any birth records," Ed said. "Or why she never turned up *any*where before now."

Sam sighed heavily. As much as he hated to admit it, the information in the report, if accurate, certainly roused his curiosity. It was odd that there was no record of Rosie's existence anywhere prior to her coming to Northaven. But it certainly didn't mean she was selling drugs. Or that she was committing any crimes, for that matter. There was still enough of the Boston vice cop lingering within him to think that maybe, just maybe, she deserved another look.

Maybe he *should* verify the information from We-FindEm.com himself, if for no other reason than to make sure the Web site wasn't peddling erroneous background checks to people like Ed who might use them to feed their erroneous assumptions. There was a good chance WeFindEm.com had made a mistake in reporting Rosie's vital statistics. And Rosie deserved to have any misinformation about herself that was floating around out there erased. She was part of what was good and decent in Northaven. She was part of what needed protecting. Sam wouldn't be doing his job if he just let this thing go as it stood.

And damned if that wasn't the finest bit of rationalizing he'd ever concocted for sticking his nose into someplace where it didn't belong.

He gazed at Ed levelly as he folded the report in half,

then quarters, and tucked it into his jacket pocket. "All right, Ed. I'll look into it. Just promise me that, from here on out, you'll stay out of it."

"Until you need me to coordinate on an investigation," the other man said.

Sam nodded reluctantly. "All right."

With any luck at all, though, it would never get that far.

3

THE MORNING FOLLOWING her sexual encounter of the baguette kind with Sam in Alice's studio, Rosie was in her not-yet-open flower shop, still thinking about him. In fact, she hadn't really stopped thinking about him during the past twenty-four hours. He might have drifted from her conscious into her subconscious from time to time—something she'd realized when she sat down to eat her dinner of bagel and Polish sausage, which she'd for sure never fixed for dinner before—but he'd always been present in her brain in some form. And his form was usually naked and sweaty when he'd been present in her brain. And he hadn't been present in just her brain, but he'd also been present in her heart. And also a couple of other body parts—at least, figuratively speaking—that she'd as soon not dwell on right now.

She sighed and brushed a hand down the front of her embroidered, dark green peasant shirt and faded blue jeans to dislodge a few remnants of dirt, but mostly all she dislodged was the shirt—over one shoulder, something it had a habit of doing thanks to its deeply scooped neckline. The spilled dirt was another by-product of thoughts about Sam, since being preoccupied was what

Rosie had been doing when she pulled a big bag of potting soil off a shelf without realizing it was open—until she'd dumped a good bit of it down the front of her clothes. Pulling her shirttail from her jeans, she shook the rest of the dirt out, not bothering to tuck the garment in again when she was done.

Oh, hang it. She wouldn't be opening for another two hours, so she had time to run to her apartment upstairs and change, once she had everything in the store set to go. All that was left to do—other than sweeping up what was left of the dirt—was to brew up and sample a new aphrodisiac tea she had blended for a client.

And, it went without saying, to think about Sam.

What was weird was that, as Rosie swept, she found herself thinking about him less in the hot, naked sex sense and more in the quiet, candlelit dinner sense. In fact, she found herself pondering the pros and cons of asking him out. Loaf of French bread aside, there had just been something about the way he'd looked at her in Alice's studio yesterday that made her think maybe, possibly, he felt steam ballooning around them, too, but was just trying to pretend he didn't.

Though why he would pretend something like that if he *was* feeling the steam was a mystery. Rosie thought she'd made clear her interest in him a long time ago. Why would a man deliberately avoid a woman who was interested in him and capable of putting a loaf of French bread in his pocket? That didn't make any sense.

Okay, so that was one con about asking him out—even if he did like her, he still might turn her down on account of that mysterious pretending the steam didn't exist thing. Pro, however, she was pretty sure he *did* like her. Con, on the other hand, if he turned her down, things between them might end up being even more awkward than they already were, and it might make for discomfort whenever their paths crossed again. And Northaven being a small town, their paths did cross fairly regularly.

Another con was that, since gossip was a popular pastime in Northaven, everyone in town would hear about the incident, and then everyone would know Rosie was jonesing for Sam. Not that she'd ever been bothered by gossip, but having it known publicly that she had tried unsuccessfully to enter the dating arena, everyone in town would suddenly want to fix her up with whatever single man they could find. Nephews. Cousins. Plumbers. Accountants. Plumbers' cousins. Plumbers' cousins' nephews. Plumbers' cousins' nephews' accountants.

In a word, oog.

Putting aside the cons, since they seemed to be piling up, Rosie considered the pros instead. Pro, if Sam agreed to go out with her, there might be some smokin' sex at the end of the evening.

Well, there you go, she thought. Pros win, hands down. Next time she saw Sam, she'd figure out some way to work an invitation to dinner or a movie—or, you know, smokin' sex—into the conversation.

When she finished sweeping, Rosie brewed up a batch of her new aphrodisiac tea. For convenience's sake, she used the teapot in the front of the shop she always kept filled with regular herbal tea for her customers, so that they could help themselves as they browsed or placed their orders. As she waited for the tea to steep, she pushed all thoughts of Sam out of her brain. It was essential that she *not* be thinking about him when she drank the tea, to ensure it worked the way it was supposed to. Thinking about Sam just naturally turned her on. He was a walking, talking aphrodisiac unto himself.

After removing the muslin pouch full of herbs from the infusion, Rosie squeezed out the last few drops and set the bag aside. Then she filled one of an assortment of earthenware mugs on the shelf beside the teapot and lifted it to her nose, inhaling deeply and smiling at the hint of cinnamon she'd added this time to give the added benefit of freshening breath. After blowing gently on the concoction, she took an experimental sip.

The taste was better than the batch she'd mixed up yesterday, thanks to the cinnamon, and she couldn't taste the kava kava now at all. But reducing the amount of kava kava might have also weakened the power of the recipe, so she'd doubled up on the damiana this time. Still, she knew she'd have to finish the entire cup and wait anywhere from fifteen to thirty minutes before she could be certain of its full effect.

She was consuming the last swallow when the bell on the front door announced the arrival of a customer, even though the store's Open-Closed sign was flipped over to the Closed position, and the hours clearly printed on the window indicated opening was nearly ninety minutes away. Stifling her irritation, Rosie turned around to politely tell the newcomer just that—

And saw Sam Maguire standing framed in the doorway, his hands hooked loosely on his hips.

The door swung closed behind him, but he took a step forward and landed in a pool of golden, early-morning sun that filtered through the window beside him. The light was almost otherworldly, lighting dark amber fires in his chocolate-brown hair and somehow softening his rugged features. Even the starkness of his white cop shirt seemed to fade to a softer cream, the sun reflecting off the gold badge pinned to his pocket and making it shine like a beacon of goodness and decency.

The look he was giving her, however, was anything but decent. His eyes were narrowed, and his lips were flattened into a tight line. But the scowl did nothing to detract from his extreme good looks, and in fact made Rosie feel kind of—

Well. There was no denying it. Either her new recipe was working way faster than she'd thought it would, or Sam Maguire's simple nearness was about to bring her to a cataclysmic orgasm. And although Rosie knew her aphrodisiac teas were good, she was pragmatic enough to realize they weren't *that* good. So she had no choice but to accept the fact that human flesh and blood would always be more powerful than plant life in bringing a woman to the brink of sexual fulfillment.

Damn, she thought. So much for not polluting the effects of the infusion with thoughts of Sam Maguire. He hadn't even said hello to her, and already her skin was growing warm—which was always her first indication that a new tea was working. The next indication was always the dampening of her palms, which—

Yep. There they went, right on cue. Except way too early for the reaction to be a result of the tea. Rosie just hoped the other kind of dampness that came next, the dampness between her legs, held off for a little while long—

Uh-oh.

Great, she thought as she vaguely registered Sam's nod and softly muttered hello. At this rate, her nipples would begin to tingle in no time fla—

Oh, yeah. There they went, too, way ahead of schedule. Maybe doubling up on the damiana hadn't been such a good idea after all....

Because it couldn't just be Sam's simple presence making her want to wrestle him to the floor the way she did just then. Could it? She always at least indulged in a little small talk before it came to that, even in her fantasies. It had to be some faster-than-usual reaction to the tea. Maybe the cinnamon and damiana worked better together than she'd realized.

"Um, hi, Chief," she said, gripping her mug tightly with both hands to keep herself from…oh, she didn't know…grabbing the placket of his shirt and ripping it down the middle, buttons flying. The top two were already undone—something that would have made her job much easier—and dark hair sprang from the opening, making her fingers itch to investigate further.

Unbidden, an image erupted in her head of him naked and prone on her bed as she dragged her fingers through the dark hair on his chest before inching them slowly, slowly, oh-so-slowly down to his flat abdomen. Then lower still, into the thatch of dark hair surrounding his cock, which she circled with sure fingers and drew eagerly toward her waiting mou—

Rosie squeezed her eyes shut tight in an effort to drive the vision out of her head. But that only made it more vivid. Because now she saw herself, too, naked and crouched over him on her hands and knees and faced in the opposite direction, with Sam gripping her hips in strong fists, his head lifted between her legs. Both of them seemed to be competing over who could consume the other first, and neither seemed to be slaking their hunger. As he hungrily ate her, she moved her head slowly up and down, pulling his big cock farther into her mouth with every descent. Immediately, Rosie snapped her eyes open again, but not before she saw the fantasy Sam's tongue dart quickly in and out of her damp—

"I'm, um…I, uh…" She tried to remember what she'd been about to say, but couldn't seem to string two thoughts, never mind two words, together. Definitely needed to lighten up on the damiana in the next recipe, she told herself. And also, the next time she mixed one up, she needed to be in a different ZIP code than Sam Maguire was in. Or maybe a different area code. Or country. Or hemisphere. Or galaxy. Yeah, that might be enough.

Finally, she managed to say, "I'm, ah, I'm actually not open yet…." Well, not her store anyway. There were other parts of her that were wide open, at least in the fantasy she couldn't seem to chase out of her brain. "I mean, I, um, I haven't even picked up my bank float for the ass register. I mean cash register," she quickly corrected herself when she realized how egregiously she'd misspoken.

"That's okay," Sam told her. Though the look he was giving her was anything but okay.

Still, she couldn't help thinking, if he wasn't going to buy anything, then he must have come here for another reason, and maybe that reason was, oh…Rosie didn't know…to have really smokin' sex.

His expression changed suddenly, to one of worry. Color her crazy, but worry didn't seem like the thing a man should be feeling if he'd just shown up for really smokin' sex.

"Are you okay, Rosie?" he asked cautiously. Caution, too, she thought, probably wasn't a good indicator of that smokin' sex thing being only minutes away. "You look a little…"

"What?" she asked.

"Distracted," he told her. Though he looked as though he'd been about to say something else. Something like, oh…Rosie didn't know…*profoundly turned-on in a way that makes me want to pull down your pants, spin you around, bend you over and bury myself inside you to the hilt.*

Oh, God…

Rosie did her best to calm herself, her thoughts and her privates. "Can I, um, can I help you, Chief?" she tried again, somehow stopping herself before uttering the entire question she'd really wanted to ask, which was *Can I help you, Chief, out of those clothes?*

"Yeah, actually, you can," he said.

Rosie knew a moment's euphoria, until she realized he wasn't talking about the clothes thing, but was simply answering the standard question of retailers everywhere.

Note to self, she thought, *doubling up on damiana makes for excellent fantasizing but it's not so good on the coherent thinking.* Or maybe it was just the way Sam Maguire was put together that made for incoherent thinking. Not to mention the *ex*cellent fantasizing.

Um, what was the question again?

Thankfully, she didn't have to remember, because Sam replied, "I need to order some flowers."

Well, hell. If he was ordering flowers, it was doubtless for a woman, and that could seriously jeopardize any asking him out on a date she might do. Worse, it could jeopardize his response to her invitation. Worst of all, it could jeopardize any potential for smokin' sex. Unless they were flowers for a funeral, she thought further, brightening. If he was going to order flowers for a dead woman, well, that was a whole 'nother ball game. Not to mention A-okay with Rosie.

"For a funeral?" she asked, hoping she didn't sound as optimistic as she felt, since that would be in really bad taste.

Sam's expression turned confused this time. "Uh, no. For my mother."

Even better, Rosie thought. Not only did it offer a new positive dimension into his character—one of caring son—but it would save her a bundle in the therapist bills she'd be paying to help her cope with her joy at hearing the news of someone else's death. Talk about a win-win situation. The only thing that might improve it would be if Sam, oh…Rosie didn't know…stepped forward and filled her mouth with his tongue, shoved one hand up her shirt to massage her breast, and thrust

the other into her pants to fondle her until she was in-
sensate with ecstasy. Other than that, the conversation
was moving along swimmingly.

Sam looked at Rosie and told himself for the tenth time
that she couldn't possibly be feeling the way she seemed
to be feeling. Surely it was just wishful thinking on his part
making her look as if she were incredibly, well…turned-
on. Because she really did seem to be incredibly, well…
turned-on. In fact, she'd been looking as if she was incredibly, well…turned-on, ever since he walked into the shop.
But there was nothing about the scenario that should have,
well…turned her on so incredibly.

She was fully clothed—except for the way her shirt
had fallen off one shoulder. One naked, ivory, luscious
shoulder. Which, in case he hadn't mentioned it, was
naked, something that pretty much indicated she wasn't
wearing anything underneath. Which meant that, under
her shirt, she was naked. And also naked. Had he mentioned she was naked under her shirt? Which was also
untucked? Something that would make it really easy for
him to scoop his hand under the garment to experience
her nakedness for himself?

A sudden, nearly overwhelming urge came over him
then to lean forward and lick her ivory, luscious—and
naked, in case that part wasn't obvious—shoulder.
Which, in turn, made him feel incredibly, well…turned-
on. God, he hoped *he* didn't look incredibly, well…
turned-on. Not the way Rosie did.

He told himself again that he was only imagining the
way she looked. How could anyone feel turned-on in her
place of employment, first thing in the morning, when,

if the broom behind her was any indication, she'd just been sweeping up? No way was sweeping a turn-on. Unless, you know, it was Rosie Bliss and her naked shoulder doing it.

Ah, hell.

His mouth and throat were starting to feel a little dry when he noticed the mug Rosie was holding in her hand. There were more like it on the shelf behind her, next to a teapot from which she had obviously just poured herself something to drink. Sam wasn't much of a tea drinker—okay, he never touched the stuff—but something wet sounded really good right then. Other than Rosie, he meant.

Damn. Then again, she did look incredibly, well… turned-on.

"Do you mind?" he said as he strode forward and reached past her for a mug.

It was a rhetorical question, naturally, since he also reached for the teapot and, without even asking for her okay, poured himself a mugful of tea. After all, there was a sign behind it that said Help Yourself, so why shouldn't he? Unless, of course, the sign referred to something other than the tea. But what were the chances Rosie had put up a sign in her shop inviting her customers to help themselves to her? Not that that probably wouldn't have been great for business.

He wasn't here for business, Sam reminded himself as he splashed tea into the mug, regardless of what he'd just said about ordering flowers for his mother. He was here to pump Rosie. Uh, for information, he meant. Only he needed to do it in a way that she wouldn't realize he was pumping her. Uh, for information, he meant. Because if he was here to actually, you know, *pump* her, she'd sure as hell know it.

He'd spent the bulk of his afternoon yesterday trying to find out more about Rosie Bliss, only to discover there was almost no information available anywhere on Rosie Bliss. Sam wasn't quite ready to throw in with Ed Dinwiddie and start suspecting her of illicit activity, but his curiosity about her had definitely been piqued. Even more so than before. He'd figured a little reconnaissance under the guise of patronizing her shop—especially at a time when it wasn't open and Rosie might be a little more relaxed—ought to lend itself to some conversation that would reveal a little more about her. Or, at the very least, give him a bit more information to go on in his search to uncover more about her. Besides, it had been a while since he'd sent his mother some flowers.

Still watching Rosie, who suddenly looked as if she were worried about something—in addition to still looking incredibly, well…turned-on—Sam started to lift the mug of tea to his lips.

But before he had a chance to taste it, she cried out, "Stop!"

Automatically, he lowered his hand. But he continued to hold her gaze steady as he asked, "Why? I thought it was for your customers."

"It is," she replied quickly.

A little too quickly to Sam's way of thinking. She seemed pretty agitated about something all of a sudden. Though she still looked very turned-on. Her pupils had expanded to the point where her green irises were mere rims around them. Her cheeks were stained with a crimson blush, and her lips looked redder than usual and were parted slightly, as if she needed more air. The skin above the low-lying neckline of her shirt was flushed, too, and something told Sam it would be hot to the touch.

The fingers of his free hand began to curl involuntarily at his side, as if they very much wanted to test that theory right now, and it was with no small effort that he managed to curb the impulse. But it rose right up again when he noticed how her chest was rising and falling rapidly, pushing her breasts against the thin fabric of her shirt. Her nipples, he couldn't possibly help noticing every time she inhaled, were hard and distended, another indication that she was indeed turned-on.

And dammit, now Sam was, too.

"Let me brew you a fresh pot," she said as she began to reach for the mug, pulling his attention—and his gaze, finally—back to the tea he'd just poured for himself. "That's been sitting there awhile."

"It's barely eight in the morning," he pointed out. "It can't have been sitting there that long. Hell, it's still hot," he added when he felt the temperature of the tea through the mug. "Besides, you obviously just had some yourself. It'll be fine."

"But you'd probably prefer coffee," she said, reaching for the mug again, moving her hand even closer.

Without asking himself why, Sam pulled the cup out of range before she could touch it. He told himself it was because he didn't like it when people made decisions for him. It wasn't because he was hoping on some level that, by removing the cup from her reach, she'd be forced to take a step forward to get it, something that would bring her body closer to his.

"It'll be fine," he repeated. "I just need a little something to quench my thirst."

"But—"

He only took a small sip first, in case the tea was hot, then, when he discovered the temperature was perfect, enjoyed a few hearty swallows. He grimaced a little when he realized it wasn't regular tea, but some herbal stuff that was a little heavy on the cinnamon. Still, it tasted fine, and it went a long way toward alleviating the dryness in his mouth.

He continued to watch Rosie as he enjoyed a few more sips, and couldn't help thinking she looked more and more panicked with every passing second. Something wasn't right with her. She just had some kind of vibe coming off her at the moment that wasn't in keeping with her usual easygoing self. And he couldn't help thinking it was his presence in her shop that was causing it.

Maybe Ed Dinwiddie was on to something, he thought before he could stop himself. Maybe everything about Rosie wasn't on the up-and-up, after all. Because somehow Sam was starting to get the impression that she'd been doing something just now, before he came into the shop, that she shouldn't have been doing. He honestly couldn't say what, but right now she seemed edgy and anxious, as if she feared she was about to be caught.

Unable to help himself—hey, you could take the cop out of vice, but you couldn't take the suspicion out of

the vice cop—he drove his gaze around the shop as sur-
reptitiously as he could, trying to discern if anything was
amiss or out of place. But the place was tidy to a fault,
and even more quaint than the police station. The dark
hardwood floor was buffed to a rich sheen, the walls
were painted forest green, striped with wooden shelves
that were overflowing with plants and flowers and pots.
An antique cash register sat on the countertop to his left,
behind which were more shelves, more plants, more
flowers, more pots. There was a door leading to a back
room that was open, and Sam could see more of the
same beyond, along with tables and stools and flower
arrangements in varying stages of completion.

For the first time, he noticed the smell of the place,
a mixture of sweet blossoms, cinnamon tea and loamy
earth. The only window was the one to the right of where
they stood, the faint golden sunlight filtering through it
the only light present at the moment. From Malcolm's
Music Mart next door, he could hear the faint strains of
something classical and heavy on the horns, music from
another time tumbling into a room that might as well
have sprung from the same century. All combined, the
impressions gave the shop an otherworldly ambiance,
where Sam could almost believe time had stopped and
he and Rosie were the only people left on the planet.

It was such a whimsical thought for such a practical
man. What the hell had come over him to make him
think like that? Shaking the odd sensations out of his
head almost literally, he downed what was left of his tea
and set the mug on a different shelf from the clean ones.
Then he looked at Rosie again.

Big mistake, he immediately realized. Because where before she had looked incredibly, well…turned-on, now, suddenly, she looked thoroughly and profoundly aroused. Not only that, but she hadn't dropped the hand with which she'd been reaching for his mug, and it still hovered near Sam's shoulder, as if she were having trouble deciding what she wanted to do with it.

And suddenly, completely unbidden, Sam had a very good idea of what she should do with it. Not only that, but he had a good idea for his own hand, too. In fact, the idea was so strong, and so demanding, he couldn't push it out of his brain. Because there, in his mind's eye, he saw himself and Rosie, standing right where they were in the middle of the flower shop, her fingers wrapped possessively around his cock as she jerked him to completion, him with his long middle finger buried in her damp slit as he drilled her for all he was worth.

And good God, where had that thought come from? he wondered as he did his best to squash it. More to the point, why wasn't it going anywhere, no matter how hard he tried to push it away?

When he opened his eyes, Sam was relieved—well, kind of—to see that Rosie had finally moved away. Well, kind of. She'd retreated a step so that her back was braced against the wall beside the shelves, and she'd dropped her hand to her side. Her eyes were fixed on his face, however, soft and liquid and still giving her the appearance of being very, very aroused. Awkwardly, hastily, she wrapped her arms tight across her midsection, as if that were the only way she could keep them to herself. But all that did was pull the fabric of her shirt taut over her breasts, something that only made her erect nipples that much more obvious.

And suddenly, her nipples weren't the only things that were erect. Sam just hoped his condition wasn't as obvious as hers.

"Flowers," he said again, turning toward a display in the front window in the hope that it might hide his own condition. Then he realized anyone walking by the shop might look in and see his condition—not that he was bragging or anything—so he turned again. But that put him right back looking at Rosie's darker-than-normal eyes. And her more-flushed-than-normal cheeks. And her fuller-than-normal mouth.

That mouth. That mouth. That ripe, erotic, luscious mouth. That mouth he wanted so desperately to cover with his own. That mouth he wanted to fill with his tongue. That mouth he wanted to feel skimming over his body, tasting him, licking him, caressing him. That mouth he wanted to see open over his member and draw him inside, slowly moving lower…lower…lower…until he disappeared completely inside it. The mouth he wanted to watch moving up and down his cock as Rosie savored every inch of him.

Damn…

As Sam looked at her and thought about her going down on him, heat began to seep through his body, until he felt as if every inch of his skin was on fire. His palms went damp, blood pooled in his groin, and his chest went as tight as a drum. He suddenly felt the way he did when he was moving behind a woman to bury himself inside her from behind—fully and profoundly aroused to the point he usually only achieved after extended foreplay with a woman. To the point where he really needed satisfaction. Painfully needed satisfaction. *Now.*

What the hell was going on?

He actually lifted a hand and began to reach for Rosie, not even sure what he intended to do. Part of him wanted to curl his fingers over one of the breasts pressing against her shirt and squeeze hard, while another part wanted to dip his hand between her legs and stroke her over the fabric of her jeans until she came in his palm. And her mouth. He wanted her mouth. He wanted his tongue in her mouth, then his cock in her mouth. And then he wanted his tongue and cock inside other parts of her, too. And he wanted…

Oh, damn, he just wanted. All of her. Right here. Right now. And he wasn't sure he'd ever be able to let her go.

"So, um, flowers?" she suddenly asked, her voice husky and breathless and low.

It took a moment for her comment to register, because Sam honestly had no idea what she was talking about. Flowers? How could she think about flowers at a time like this? Hell, he couldn't think about anything but peeling off every scrap of clothing she was wearing and taking her right there on the floor of her shop. There was no way he could think about anything when he was this turned-on. Except for, you know, peeling off every scrap of clothing Rosie was wearing and taking her right there on the floor of her shop.

"Flowers?" he repeated, puzzled.

She nodded, a jerky, anxious gesture. "Yeah. Flowers. You said you needed to order some for your mother."

The reminder of his mother should have been like a bucket of ice water hurled onto his libido. There was just nothing like the introduction of a woman who surpassed even June Cleaver and Marion Cunningham on the Ultimate Mom Scale to wither a man's desire like *that*. But Sam's cock barely dipped in response. He told himself to get out of the store, to hie himself home where he could take care of his condition himself and then return to work. But if he bolted like that, it might make Rosie suspicious, and he wanted her to be relaxed, because he really needed to seduce her.

Question her, he quickly corrected himself. He needed to question her. At least, he thought he did. Wasn't that why he'd come into the shop in the first place? He couldn't remember now. Though he was pretty sure it had been because he needed to question her. About…something. Something really important. Something that was right there at the edge of his brain….

"Is it a special occasion?" Rosie asked.

Before he could stop himself, Sam shook his head. Not a special occasion, he thought, but something that sort of sounded like occasion. Copulation? Fornication? Procreation…?

Investigation! That was it. He was supposed to be investigating something. Something that had to do with… What was his job again? Chief of police, he remembered. That's right. He was chief of police, which meant he was investigating… Crime! That was it. He investigated crime. And Rosie's crime was…

He looked at her again. Well, it was criminal the way she made him feel at the moment, he thought. But he couldn't exactly arrest her for that. So it must have been something else….

Out of nowhere, Ed Dinwiddie's face swam up in Sam's brain, and that, if nothing else, went a long way toward sending his staff to half-mast. Oh, yeah, he recalled when blood finally began to flow into his other head—the one he *should* be thinking with. He was supposed to be investigating Rosie on suspicion of drug trafficking.

Which, of course, he didn't believe for a moment she was engaged in, but he'd promised Ed he'd look into it. If nothing else, Sam needed to prove to the other man once and for all that Rosie Bliss wasn't peddling dope on the Northaven campus. Sam didn't know what she *was* doing—other than making him profoundly and fully aroused…at least until thoughts of Ed intruded—but it wasn't peddling dope on the Northaven campus. And to prove that to Ed, Sam had decided to feel Rosie up…ah, feel her *out*…by coming into her shop on the ruse of buying flowers for his mother at a time when she would be alone and relaxed, with her pants down. Her *guard* down, he hastily amended. At a time when she'd have her guard down.

It was all coming back to him now.

"So you're just sending your mother flowers for no reason?" she asked. "What a good son you are."

No, he was sending flowers to his mother in an effort to lull Rosie into a false sense of security so he could mislead her. What a rotten son of a bitch he was.

"Well, it's been a while," he said. Then, to avoid any further delving into his own personal life, since he was much more interested in delving into Rosie…ah, into Rosie's life, he meant, he hastily added, "What? You don't send your mother flowers for no reason? I'd think a florist would do that sort of thing all the time."

Sam had thought the question would be an innocuous way to change the subject—and also bring some relief to a certain part of his anatomy that could really use relieving right now. Relieving that *didn't* involve oral sex, he meant. He hadn't realized his question would instead drop the temperature in the room a good eight hundred degrees. Celsius, at that. Which pretty much took care of that relieving business. Without even meaning to, Sam had effectively doused *both* their libidos with ice water.

"No," Rosie said coolly as she pushed herself away from the wall and made her way toward the counter on the other side of the room. "I don't send my mother flowers."

Before Sam could comment further, she was pulling a thick catalog from one of the shelves behind the cash register, which she opened onto the counter and began to flip through.

"There are some lovely arrangements in here," she said in the same chilly tone of voice, further easing Sam's discomfort. "But if you'd prefer something more personal, with flowers you've chosen yourself, I'll do my best to accommodate you."

Sam had always thought Rosie had a great voice, rich and full and whiskey-rough at times, and filled with barely restrained good humor. At the moment, however, her words were clipped and cold and caustic. And he couldn't for the life of him figure out what had generated the sudden change. Not that he wasn't grateful for the arctic turn of events, since it was working wonders on quashing his arousal, but to see Rosie go so quickly from one extreme to the other was more than a little disconcerting.

It also made him that much more curious about her.

"Did I say something I shouldn't have?" he asked.

Her head snapped up at that, and for a moment, she only glared at him. Then she seemed to realize how unfairly she was treating him, and she visibly relaxed.

"I'm sorry," she apologized with genuine regret. "It's just that…" She sighed heavily and straightened, dragging a hand through the loose hair framing her face. "My mother and I…don't exactly get along."

"Ah," Sam said. Then, hoping he sounded nonchalant, just making conversation, that's all, he added, "How long has that been going on?"

For a moment, he didn't think she was going to answer him. Then, softly, she said, "Almost two decades."

He arched his eyebrows at that. "Rough adolescence?"

She barked out a single, nervous laugh at that, then slapped a hand over her mouth to prevent any further outburst. "Um, you might say that," she told him when she dropped her hand to the counter again. Quickly, before he had a chance to jump on the remark, she pointed down to the catalog and hurried on, "This is one of my favorite arrangements for mothers. And it's reasonably priced. What do you think?"

Sam did his best to look casual as he made his way across the room. But instead of stopping on the opposite side of the counter, where he figured customers were supposed to stay, he sauntered behind it to stand next to

Rosie. This time she was the one to arch her eyebrows as he came to a halt beside her, but she didn't tell him to move his butt back to the other side of the counter where it belonged.

"That's nice," Sam said. "But she really likes daisies. Those big pink ones."

"Gerbera?"

"I guess that's what they are. Do you have anything like that?"

"Sure."

She flipped through a few more pages, and as she did, Sam watched her face. Her skin was flawless, the hint of a blush still staining her cheeks. Her lashes were darker than her hair, long and thick and completely devoid of mascara. In fact, as far as he could tell, she wasn't wearing any makeup at all. Usually, Sam didn't go for the organic types. Usually, he liked his women to rejoice in their femininity and exploit it to the fullest extent. He liked women who wore a lot of makeup and few clothes. Who staggered around on mile-high heels and puffed up their hair to maximum height.

Which made his response to Rosie—especially the one that still lingered in his brain…and, oh, all right, his groin—all the more puzzling. There was absolutely nothing provocative about her at the moment. Yet he still had the urge to lean forward and run his open mouth along the back of her neck.

"Perfect," she said.

His gaze still pinned to the spot where her nape flowed into her shoulder, Sam murmured, before he could stop himself, "It sure is."

He didn't realize he'd spoken the observation aloud until his view of her neck was obscured by her hand. That was when he shifted his gaze to her face and saw Rosie staring back at him. Neither of them spoke for a moment—which, on Sam's part, at least, was because he couldn't think of a single thing to say…except maybe, "Nice neck." And in that moment, he feared Rosie was going to come down on him for sexually harassing her. Though he would have begged to differ, since all he was doing was admiring something way more beautiful than the flower arrangement in the photo to which she'd tried to direct his attention. Then she smiled at him. A soft, gentle, downright sweet smile that shouldn't have set off any alarms in his head.

But it did. Big-time.

He realized why when she suddenly asked, "Chief… I mean, Sam…are you busy Friday night?"

So caught off-guard was he, Sam could only reply, "Busy? Friday? Night?"

Rosie nodded. "It's the funniest thing. Just before you came in this morning, I was trying to think of some way to ask you out. And now, for some reason…" She lifted her shoulder—that creamy, flawless, naked shoulder that was peeking out from her shirt again—and let it drop. "For some reason, the time seems right."

Oh, this was the last thing he needed, Sam thought. To go out on a date with Rosie Bliss. Not just because he feared he might not be able to battle another case of out-and-out arousal like the one he was still battling—and he tried not to think about what a disgrace to his gender that made him, *fearing* another episode like that, never mind *battling* it—but because he was skirting the lines of an investigation into her background and her activities.

No, she wasn't officially under investigation for anything. He couldn't even say for sure she was under suspicion of anything. But she did have his interest. Well, in a way that *didn't* include getting into her pants. Though the thought of that was certainly interesting, too....

Nevertheless, thanks to Ed Dinwiddie, Sam was currently in a position that could be compromised if he had anything to do with Rosie that was in the slightest bit social, never mind romantic. If he went out with her on a date while he was looking into her background, it would fall onto the "unethical" side of the blurry line he was toeing at the moment.

No matter how badly he might want to go out with her on a date.

Later, he told himself. After he'd proved to Ed Dinwiddie that Rosie was a decent, law-abiding citizen. Then maybe the two of them could—

Nothing, he told himself adamantly. He and Rosie could do nothing. She was much too nice a woman for a man like him to get involved with. Even if the way she made him feel lately was anything *but* nice. Well, okay, it *was* nice, the way she made him feel. Really nice, matter of fact. Too nice. It just wasn't, you know, *nice* for him to feel that way about her. On account of she was too nice for a man like him, who didn't deserve nice, to have feelings that nice about her.

"Uh, Rosie," he said before realizing he had absolutely no idea what to say.

But she spoke at the same time, sounding a little

nervous now as she asked, "So how about it? You want to have dinner Friday night? Maybe go to a movie? Unless you've already seen the only two showing in town," she added with a smile that was a little too bright. "That's one thing about small-town life I don't guess I'll ever get used to," she added way too matter-of-factly. "I'm a city girl, born and bred, so I'm just not used to the dearth of movie theaters. And nightclubs. And restaurants. And bars. And shopping malls. Well, I'm sure you sympathize, having moved here from Boston. Not that I want to imply you don't like living here. Or that I don't, either, for that matter. Because I do. I like it very much. It's just a lot different from where I grew up and what I'm used to and how I—"

She dropped her face into her hands. "And oh, my God, I sound like such a jerk," she finally concluded.

Before Sam had a chance to disagree, she scrubbed her hands over her face as if she were trying to erase signs of anything she may have said or done since he entered the store, and raised her head again. She sighed heavily and smiled again, this time looking a little more like herself.

"Anyway," she tried again, "what do you say? You doing anything Friday night?"

What he wouldn't have given to be able to say yes. Except that instead of going out, he'd suggest they stay in. Someplace intimate and isolated where there was no chance of anyone disturbing them while they explored more fully—over and over and over again—whatever this weird, steamy thing was that had come over them this morning.

Instead, he told her, "I'm actually busy Friday night." And he made a mental note to schedule something for Friday night.

She looked confused for a minute, then embarrassed, then hurt. Then she pasted on a smile that was a little too happy. "Oh. Okay. Well, then. Maybe some other time."

Sam made himself nod and tried not to feel like a complete bastard. "Yeah. Maybe some other time." And then, pretending he wasn't a complete bastard, he added, "Now about those flowers for my mother…"

4

ROSIE DID HER BEST to remain professional as she rang up Sam's purchase, pretending she didn't feel like a complete moron for having so baldly asked him to go out with her. But when she'd glanced up from the catalog to see him looking at her neck with such undisguised longing, and when she'd seen reflected in his eyes the same acute desire she felt for him shining back at her, she'd figured he'd been feeling the same heat burning up the air between them that she did, and she'd been sure he would accept her invitation. When he'd declined instead, she'd felt as if someone had slipped a sardine down the back of her shirt, so keen had been her surprise—and so sharp had been her disappointment.

Yeah, yeah, yeah, there was that small matter of him having drunk a cup of her aphrodisiac tea, which was probably the only thing that had caused him to be ogling her neck in the first place, thereby making any attraction he might have felt for her a falsely manufactured one, so she should be happy he had turned her down, anyway. So why wasn't she happy about that?

Maybe because she was confident that, ultimately,

his reaction to her hadn't been caused by the tea any more than her reaction to him had been. Probably. There hadn't been enough time for either of them to have been affected. Probably. Therefore anything either of them had felt must have been a natural response to a genuine attraction. Probably. So if Sam had turned her down, it wasn't because he wasn't attracted to her. Probably. It was because he just didn't want to go out with her. Probably.

Now as she returned his credit card and presented his receipt for his signature, she managed to say, "I'm sure your mother will love the flowers. It's nice of you to send them to her for no reason like that. You really are a good son."

He shrugged off the compliment as he signed the receipt and tucked the credit card back into his wallet. "If I were a good son, I'd drive down to Boston and deliver them to her myself. But I just can't get away right now."

Interesting, Rosie thought. She had the opposite problem. She had plenty of time when she could travel if she wanted to. But she was way too scared to go anywhere.

"So you being a city girl," Sam continued, "did you move to Northaven from Boston, too?"

Rosie's eyes went wide at the question. When had she told him she was a city girl? Immediately, she recalled her babbling episode right after asking him out. Oh, damn. She couldn't believe she'd revealed something like that about herself. She was always so careful to be close-lipped about her past. The queen of evasion and champion of the sidestep rhumba, that was Rosie.

No one in Northaven knew anything about what had happened to her when she was a kid living in Miami, or later when she was a young woman living in Boulder. And no one ever would find out about all that. Her very life could depend on keeping that secret.

Even if Rosie hadn't told Sam specifically what city she called her hometown, what little she'd said could potentially reveal something about who she really was and what she'd been once upon a time. Especially to a man like him, whose job revolved around collecting clues and solving mysteries. She couldn't have anyone knowing who she really was and what she'd been once upon a time. Not even Sam.

Especially not Sam.

"No, not Boston," she told him. "I'm not from *that* big a city."

Because hey, when you considered Miami proper versus Boston proper, Boston was way bigger. It was just that Miami was so spread out geographically. Never mind the fact that the metropolitan areas of both cities were probably virtually identical. And certainly the urbanism of both was comparable. Rosie had learned a long time ago that considering specifics and speaking in literal terms went a long way when one was trying to hide one's identity.

"So where are you from?" Sam asked.

Clearly, he wasn't going to let it go. She told herself to lie to him. That's what she usually did when pressed for details about her past. When it was a matter of survival, ethics didn't really come into play very often. Or, um, at all.

In spite of that, she still tried to be truthful by telling him, "Actually, I grew up in the south."

He looked surprised. "You don't have a Southern accent."

"Well, it's been a while since I lived there."

"How long?"

"Years," she said.

"How many years?"

She smiled, hoping the gesture looked flirtatious and not annoyed. "A lot of years."

He smiled back. And his smile definitely looked flirtatious. And also annoyed. "What part of the South? I've never visited down there."

"It's beautiful. You should definitely plan a trip sometime," she said, using his remark as an opportunity to try and change the subject.

"Don't try and change the subject," he said, his smile growing broader. "Where'd you grow up?"

She blew out an exasperated sound, but continued to smile at him, this time with resignation. "You know, for a guy who doesn't want to go out with me, you sure seem to be trying to get to know me better."

"I never said I didn't want to go out with you," he told her after only a small hesitation. "I just said I'm busy Friday night, that's all."

She nibbled her lower lip as she tried to figure out what that meant, and Sam's gaze immediately flew to her mouth. His eyes grew darker, his lips parted, and Rosie suddenly felt as if she'd just downed a whole gallon of her latest aphrodisiac tea. She was definitely going to have to double-check just how much damiana had found its way into that last batch. Because she was beginning to think maybe, in a momentary lapse, she'd accidentally included an entire crop.

What the hell, she thought. Might as well go for broke. "Then what are you doing Saturday night?" she asked.

He met her gaze levelly, and for some reason, in spite of what he'd just said, Rosie got the impression he was trying to think of some way to turn her down again.

Instead, his smile returned, and he told her, "I guess I'll be picking you up around seven. Be thinking about what you'd like to do."

And with that, he tucked his receipt into his wallet, folded it closed and returned it to the back pocket of his trousers. He lifted two fingers to his forehead in farewell, then spun around and made his way out the door. Leaving Rosie to wonder just who had asked out whom, and thinking about all the things she wanted to do—mostly to Sam—Saturday night.

The bell on the door rang merrily as he opened it and stepped through it. "Have a nice day," Rosie said as he exited. And then, when the door was closed behind him, she added a little more softly, "And do come again. Soon."

INSTEAD OF RETURNING to the station after leaving Rosie's shop, as Sam knew he should—and not just because he wanted to see what he could uncover about her with that little bone she'd thrown him about being from a big city in the South…if that was even true—he headed in the opposite direction, away from town and toward home. His house was only a few blocks from the station, so he always walked to and from work, but today, he wanted to run. Fast.

In fact, he felt like entering a marathon. Preferably one that would take him thousands of miles away from where he was now. Someplace where it was really cold. Land o' Cold Lakes. That was where he wanted to be. Or, at the very least, Land o' Cold Showers. But since no such place existed, he'd just have to make do with House o' Cold Showers. In this case, his house. Because Sam still had a boner the size of a Louisville Slugger, thanks to the way he'd been feeling in Rosie's shop— and continued to feel now.

What the *hell* had just happened in Rosie's shop? How could he have been so completely, thoroughly turned-on simply by being in her presence? To the point where, for a while there, he would have been hard-pressed to remember his own name.

He was still pondering the questions—without answers to any of them—as he cut across the town square toward Division Street. He told himself his memory of his feelings must be exaggerated, that he couldn't possibly have wanted her with the immediacy and intensity he recalled. But hell, he was still physically aroused this long after the fact, so he must have been powerfully turned-on, just by her simple nearness. He could still smell the scent of her—that rich, earthy aroma—could still see the blush of her desire darkening the flesh above her shirt. He could still hear the way her breathing had come in ragged, rapid bursts, could fairly taste the expanse of her neck he'd so wanted to savor. He tried to remember when the situation had changed from inquisitive to incandescent, but all he could recall was how much he'd wanted Rosie, and how she'd

seemed to want him, too, with a passion as unbridled—
and unexpected—as his own.

It didn't make any sense. Yeah, he'd always found her
attractive, and, all modesty aside, he knew she was attracted to him. But there had been no precedent for the
heat they'd just generated in her shop. A few assessing
looks from time to time, maybe. And okay, once, when
he shook her hand after an introduction, Sam had held
it a little longer than he needed to. And, yeah, she'd
touched him on the arm or shoulder a couple of times
when speaking to him. All had been fairly innocuous
gestures. How had things gone from innocent to incen-
diary in no time flat?

He told himself to stop trying to understand that and
start focusing on figuring out what he should do next.
How was he going to handle his date with Rosie
Saturday night when he never should have agreed to go
out with her in the first place?

A half hour later, he still wasn't sure what to do about
his date with Rosie, but he'd at least taken care of his
Louisville Slugger problem in the shower. Under other
circumstances, the prospect of going out with her might
have actually been kind of nice. If *she* wasn't so nice,
he meant. And if she *wasn't* nice, then it *really* would
have been nice to go out with her. Because then the two
of them might have a chance to further explore the
sudden heat arcing between them. As it was, Sam was
going to have to keep his hands to himself Saturday
night. And not just because Rosie was such a nice
woman. But because of the very unnice thing he was
about to do to her.

After changing into a fresh uniform of white shirt and brown trousers, he went to look for his old address book. His house was a modest bungalow built just after the first World War, with a big kitchen, dining room and living room, since those were the rooms people used the most in those days. The two bedrooms were smaller, which was fine with him, since he didn't spend a lot of time in them anyway—more was the pity sometimes. In fact, he'd turned one of them into a home office, and it was to that room he went now.

Like the rest of the house, the furnishings were minimal and masculine—and in no way quaint, by God. Even if the hardwood floors creaked comfortably whenever he tread upon them and his housekeeper had made curtains for all the windows, insisting no home should be without them. The entire place was painted off-white—no Wedgwood blue, by God—and he'd stripped and stained the trim back to its natural mahogany. There were no frilly rugs like you saw in the Spiegel catalog, no knickknacks and bric-a-brac or any other cute-named accessories to clutter things up. Only clean lines and blunt angles and neutral colors. The way Sam liked to keep his life, too, come to think of it.

He found his address book with little trouble, since it, like so much of his life in Boston, was still packed away in a box and stowed in the closet. He spoke to his former colleagues in the city with some regularity, enough so that he didn't need to look up their numbers. But during his years as a vice cop, Sam had made a handful of contacts in other cities, as well, especially those that saw heavy drug traffic. New York. Philadelphia. Los Angeles. Miami. He knew vice detectives in a few other cities, as well, including some in the South, like Atlanta and Nashville.

It was to those two and Miami to which he turned his attention now, thanks to their geographic locations below the Mason-Dixon line. He knew Doreen McCabe still worked Atlanta Vice, and he was reasonably sure Stu Dorfman was still on the Miami force. He'd have to double-check whether or not Paul Gatling had asked for that transfer to homicide in Nashville, but even if the other man was in a different department now, he could direct Sam to someone else in Nashville Vice.

Sam still wasn't sure what he was going to ask for when he started to punch the buttons of Paul's phone number first. Maybe just have all three detectives run Rosie's name through their systems, to see what—if anything—came up. And he'd contact the Massachusetts DMV to get a copy of her driver's license photo. Maybe e-mail that to each of them, too. And it wouldn't hurt to get her social security number and run that, as well.

He told himself he wasn't investigating her, because he wasn't. Not really. She was what the guys in vice used to call "a person of interest." A person who might know something of value without even realizing it. A person who might be able to lead them to someone else. A person who may or may not be an accessory to a crime.

It wasn't an investigation, he told himself again as he thumbed the last number of Paul's extension in Nashville. He just found Rosie…interesting.

He'd halfway expected to get Paul's voice mail, but the guy picked up on the second ring, barking out, "Gatling."

"Paul," Sam said by way of a greeting. "Sam

Maguire. Boston Vice. Well, formerly Boston Vice," he quickly corrected himself.

"Sam!" the other man cried with immediate recognition and obvious delight. "Long time, no hear from. But what's with the formerly crap? You're not with vice anymore? Why not? You going soft?"

Sam chuckled, but didn't feel particularly jovial. He wasn't soft, dammit. He was jaded. Big difference. "Took another job," he told Paul. "I'm chief of police now."

"In Boston?" Paul asked incredulously.

"Ah, no," Sam told him. "A little farther north. Small town."

"Woooo," Paul replied with all the enthusiasm of an eighth-grader. "He's hit the big time now. Chief of Cabot Cove PD."

"Not that much farther north," Sam said, gritting his teeth at the *Murder, She Wrote* reference. Northaven was nothing like Jessica Fletcher's little burg. It was way more saccharine than that.

"Look, I need some help with a local matter," Sam hurried on before Paul could pry too much. The last thing he wanted to tell a former colleague was that he was now responsible for keeping the peace in places like Brenda's Bed and Bath, Jerry's Java Hut, Helen's House of Hairdos and Patty's Pet Palace.

"If it's a local matter, why are you calling me?" Paul asked.

"Because the woman involved moved here from somewhere else."

"Nashville?" the other man concluded for obvious reasons.

"I don't know," Sam confessed. "I only know she's from a metropolitan area in the South."

The other man laughed. "Oh, yeah, that narrows it down. Can't be more than fifteen or twenty metropolitan areas in the South. You Yankees. Think you've got a monopoly on urban life. Next you'll be asking me why I don't drive down to New Orleans for some gumbo for dinner, since it can't be more than an hour's drive from Nashville."

"You mean it's not?" Sam asked.

His response from the other end of the line was dead silence.

So Sam replied, "Oh. Well, I stand corrected."

Paul growled something unintelligible from his seat that was clearly more than an hour's drive from New Orleans. "What's the name of the suspect?" he asked.

Sam opened his mouth to tell Paul Rosie wasn't a suspect, but couldn't quite push the words out. As much as he kept insisting she wasn't a suspect, he *was* a little suspicious of her. Otherwise he wouldn't be calling people like Paul. And maybe if Paul thought she was a wanted woman—well, wanted for something other than what Sam wanted her for—he might be more inclined to be thorough.

So he hedged, "The woman's name is Rosie Bliss. But Rosie may be a nickname. Might want to look under Rose Bliss, too. Or Rosemary. Or Roseanne. Or Rosalie. Or any other variation you can think of."

"Hang on a minute while I look for my baby name book, will ya?" Paul asked wryly. "I know it was here a minute ago."

"Just trying to be helpful, Paul."

"Yeah, 'cause God knows it never would've occurred to me. Got her social?" he asked further, before Sam could apologize, clearly not needing an apology, since vice cops sniped at each other on a fairly regular basis. Like constantly.

"Not yet," Sam said, "but I'll send it to you as soon as I do. Along with her photo," he added, intuiting the other man's next question. "Gimme your e-mail address." After jotting it down, Sam continued, "Look for both this afternoon. Right now, I'm just looking for…" What? he asked himself. "Anything you might have on the name."

"You thinking it's an alias?"

Well, not until that moment, Sam hadn't been. Man, maybe you could take the vice cop out of the detective if you put him someplace like Northaven. "I don't know," he said honestly.

"Why the interest?" Paul asked. "What's she done? I mean, I'm assuming she's a suspect, right?"

"Well, not really," Sam conceded reluctantly.

"Not really?" the other man repeated dubiously.

Sam didn't blame him. *Not really* wasn't the sort of answer you heard when you worked vice. It was generally either *yes* or *no*. Narcotics, gambling and prostitution didn't tend to have too many shades of gray.

"She's a person of interest," Sam said.

"So then she *is* a suspect," Paul concluded. Since—*all right*—the term "person of interest" was also code for "person suspected of a crime," even though we can't prove it yet, which is why the person is interesting—duh.

"She's a person of interest," Sam repeated. "Let's just leave it at that for now."

"Okay, guy, whatever you say. She's your suspect."

Sam expelled a restless sigh and ran a hand through his hair. She wasn't a suspect, he told himself again. But she certainly was something.

Not the least of which was his date for Saturday night.

BY SATURDAY AFTERNOON, Sam had heard back from all three of his colleagues, but not one of them had been able to uncover anything about Rosie prior to her appearance in Northaven. Which would have been reassuring had it not been for the fact that not one of them had been able to uncover anything about Rosie prior to her appearance in Northaven. No record of employment. No record of residency. No record of ever having applied for a driver's license, credit card, bank loan or mortgage or lease. And there should have been records of all of those things. But Rosie Bliss didn't appear anywhere—in the south, north, east *or* west—until her arrival in Northaven, Massachusetts two years ago.

Even more interesting—Sam hesitated to use the word *suspicious,* even though it was that and more—was that her social security number hadn't been recorded on any documents prior to her moving to Northaven. No educational institutions, no medical records, no voter registrations. It also began with numbers indicating she was born in Massachusetts, not the South. So either Rosie was lying about where she was from, or Rosie had forged her credentials. Or Rosie was lying about where she was from *and* forged her credentials. Any way Sam looked at it, something about Rosie didn't fit.

Had it not been for the nonexistence of records, her evasiveness about where she had come from wouldn't have really bothered him. He would have simply concluded that she had moved from one place to another to start her life over, as so many people did. Maybe when she moved here two years ago, she'd been coming off a bad experience—say a bitter divorce or the death of a loved one—and, not wanting to dwell on the past, had kept that past to herself and created a different one to tell her new neighbors. She might have even legally changed her name, which would explain why Rosie Bliss—in any variation—hadn't come up on any records checks.

There was nothing wrong with any of that, of course. Hell, Sam hadn't exactly been forthcoming and gregarious about his own past since moving here. Of course, he hadn't been tempted to change his name. And he for sure hadn't created a phony baloney social security number for himself.

And that was what was most troubling about all those nondiscoveries of Rosie's existence. It wasn't that she had committed the crime of identity theft, because the social security number she was using hadn't been stolen from someone else. It simply didn't show up on the books anywhere until it showed up in Northaven as belonging to Rosie Bliss.

Sam supposed it was possible she had moved here from another country and become a naturalized citizen—she hadn't, after all, said exactly *what* south she was from. Could be the south of France or the south of

Sweden or the south of Antarctica for all he knew. But there was no record of naturalization proceedings for her, either. No, Rosie Bliss might as well have just materialized out of thin air two years ago.

Seated at the desk in his house, Sam tossed down the pen with which he'd been doodling as he spoke to Doreen McCabe in Atlanta about Rosie. Not much to his surprise, he realized he'd doodled a woman's naked torso with larger-than-average breasts, like Rosie's. Which was strange, since he had no idea what hers looked like, even having ogled her on more than one occasion.

Three days had passed since he had seen her—days he'd made damned sure he didn't run into her—and he could still see, hear and smell her, the way she'd been in her shop that morning, looking so thoroughly turned-on. Her scent, especially, had haunted him, that dark fragrance of her musky arousal—which he told himself he must have imagined—mixed with the sweet smell of the flowers. Not a night had passed when he hadn't dreamed of her, not a day had passed when he hadn't thought of her. And although he should have been pondering the mysteries of her origins and why she'd appeared out of nowhere, instead he'd been dreaming about how it would be once they were together again.

What did she expect of the evening ahead? he wondered. What did he? If things between them turned romantic—or even sexual—what was he supposed to do? He still wasn't convinced she had committed a crime. There could still be a logical explanation for her sudden appearance out of nowhere. Even if he didn't suspect her of any wrongdoing, he was still beginning to wonder if there was *some*thing about her that just wasn't…right.

So that was his answer, then. Tonight, what should happen between them was nothing. Nothing more than the two of them going out to have a nice time, then parting ways at evening's end with a fond farewell and some vague plan to do it again real soon, which, of course, Sam would never act on. Even more significant than the fact that Rosie was a person of interest was the fact that she was a person of niceness. And nice had no place in the life of a man like Sam. He had a habit of turning nice into tragedy. Hell, he had a way of turning nice into dead.

So whatever happened tonight with Rosie, at the end of it, he'd go home alone. The way he deserved to be.

As THE SECOND HAND of the clock on her nightstand neared the twelve for the fifth time since she'd been watching it, Rosie inhaled a deep breath, counted slowly to ten, and exhaled again. There. Five minutes of slow, deep breathing. No matter how stressed-out or wound-up she got, that always calmed her down nicely. Of course, she wasn't normally stressed-out or wound-up about the prospect of going out with Sam Maguire, especially after inadvertently drugging him with her aph-rodisiac tea, so—

Damn. Now she was all stressed-out and wound-up again.

She reminded herself that she had *not* drugged Sam Maguire, even if he'd seemed really, really, really turned-on in her shop the other morning. Not only was her tea *not* a drug, but even if he *had* drunk a cup, there hadn't been time for him to be affected by it. Of course, she'd been sure there hadn't been enough time for *her* to be affected by it, either, and she'd had the most extreme reaction to the concoction that she'd ever had before.

Then again, it probably wasn't her *concoction* that had caused that, so much as Sam's unmistakably erect *co—*

Oh, hell. Now she was aroused again.

She muttered a ripe curse under her breath and wondered if she had time for five more minutes of deep breathing. Not unless Sam was ten minutes late, she thought as she looked at the clock. It was five till seven, and she was still in her underwear. Granted, it was very nice underwear—a caramel-colored, translucent demi-bra and matching thong—but she supposed she should put on the rest of her clothes before she answered the front door if she didn't want to end up on the porch coupling madly with Sam. That might cause tongues to wag. And it might make people gossip, too.

Quickly, she shimmied into a sleeveless black cotton sheath and threw a dark red cardigan on over it, hoping the ensemble would be either casual enough or dressy enough for the evening ahead. She wasn't sure where she and Sam would be going, in spite of being the one who'd initially issued the invitation for a date. She supposed she could have called him and asked, but she'd done her best to avoid him for the past few days, since she hadn't been sure what to say to a man with whom she'd shared a very nice morning, ah…sexual arousal. Not that she had any idea what to say to him tonight, either. Other than "Sink your teeth into my sweet honeypot, baby." That probably wouldn't happen until *after* dinner.

Oh, God, now she was aroused *again*. She had to stop thinking about Sam in solely sexual terms. This was just a date, she reminded herself. The two of them had that whole getting-to-know-you phase to wade through before they could even think about making their relationship physical. Hell, they didn't even *have* a relationship to *make* physical. Yeah, okay, so she'd been thinking in terms of smokin' sex when she'd decided to ask him out. And okay, she wasn't exactly a shrinking violet when it came to men. She'd been around the block. More than once. In several cities. If the opportunity to indulge in wild monkey love tonight presented itself, she couldn't say she would decline.

Hah, she immediately thought. Wouldn't decline? She'd be on Sam like white on rice.

Still, it had been a long time since she'd been with anyone. And for all she knew, Sam wasn't the kind of man who jumped into the sack with any available woman, just for the sake of scratching a sexual itch. She doubted it, but it was possible. She couldn't assume tonight would end in smokin' sex. No matter how much she might want it to.

She fastened a thin gold chain around her throat and was clipping gold hoops onto her ears when the doorbell rang, right on time. She took a few seconds to inhale a half-dozen deep breaths, but all that did was make her dizzy. So after smoothing a hand over the front of her dress one final time, Rosie grasped the doorknob and twisted, pulling the door toward herself.

She hadn't thought it would be possible for Sam Maguire to look better than he did in his cop duds. But dressed in softly faded blue jeans, a white oxford shirt with dark gray pinstripes, and a charcoal blazer, he was beyond dreamy.

Rosie's front door was actually in the back of the building at the top of a flight of wooden stairs, since her apartment was over her shop, so she was virtually eye level with the sun sinking low beneath the trees behind him. Above it, the sky was stained a rich purpling blue, streaked with faint traces of orange and gold. With his flawless good looks and deep-set eyes, for one scant instance, Sam looked like a Renaissance seraph, right down to the hazy sunset halo. But she suspected rather strongly that he was no angel.

And that was a Very Good Thing.

In one hand, he held a small box of chocolates, which he extended a little awkwardly toward her. "I was going to bring you flowers," he said by way of a greeting, "but since there's only one florist in town, they wouldn't have been much of a surprise. I figure you can't go wrong with chocolate."

"You figure right," she said as she accepted the gift from him, suddenly feeling a little shy for no reason she could name. "Thanks."

"You're welcome."

She gestured vaguely over her shoulder with her thumb. "Do you want to come in for a little while first? I mean, I don't know what you have planned, but we could start with a glass of wine if you want."

He didn't reply right away, and in fact looked at her

as somberly as he might were he trying to decide the fate of the world. Finally, he said, "Sure. We don't have to be anywhere right away. A glass of wine would be nice."

"Red or white?" she asked as she stepped aside for him to enter. Oh, God, she hoped the entire evening wouldn't be made up of chitchat.

"Red," he said as she closed the door behind him.

He immediately looked out of place in her apartment, much too masculine for her overstuffed sofa in peachy chintz and the soft, fat club chair in sage-green damask. The area rugs scattered over the hardwood floor were mixed but complementary Orientals in gauzy pastel shades, and her collection of dozens of crystal candlesticks was scattered on the mantelpiece behind him. The two lamps had tasseled shades and the coffee table was a Queen Anne reproduction with curvy legs. All of it was housed within walls the color of a summer twilight. Rosie had always thought the room was fairly gender neutral. Now, she saw that it was hopelessly feminine. How odd that she only realized that with Sam standing in the middle of it all.

He didn't follow her to the kitchen when she went to retrieve the wine, and she wasn't sure what to make of that. Could mean he was trying to be polite and wait for an invitation. Could mean he was feeling awkward around her and still needed some space. Could mean he'd changed his mind about going out with her and planned to flee the moment her back was turned.

Or it could mean he wanted to snoop, she thought further when she returned to her living room to find him going through the drawer of the small writing desk that was tucked into the corner near the fireplace.

She halted in the doorway, knowing the floorboards would creak when she strode across the room, and not wanting to alert him to her presence. He was definitely looking for something, sifting through stationery, stamps, return address labels and a handful of as-yet-to-be-paid bills. Though what that might be, she couldn't have said.

Finally, she asked, "Can I help you?"

He spun quickly around to look at her, and there was no mistaking his expression. Guilty, guilty, guilty. For all of a nanosecond. Then his face changed completely. He straightened slowly and smiled easily, even a little sheepishly. "Yeah, a pen," he said. "I needed to write myself a note, and mine's not working."

To illustrate the fact—and, Rosie couldn't help thinking, try to exonerate himself—he lifted a small notebook he'd obviously retrieved from his jacket and clicked a pen, scribbling on the paper to show her that no ink was coming out.

"I always have to write down reminders to myself," he added, "or I forget the things I need to do. And I just now remembered a phone call I have to make tomorrow."

His explanation made perfect sense, and the pen clearly was out of ink. So why was Rosie having trouble believing him? There was just something in his posture that wasn't right. But then, why would he be rifling through her desk if he *wasn't* looking for a pen?

"Try the drawer to the right of the one you're—" she bit off the words *rifling through* and instead said "—searching. There should be a couple in there."

"Great," he said before turning back around to do just that.

Rosie crossed the room and waited until he'd finished jotting down his note to himself before handing him his wine.

"I like your apartment," he told her after he tucked his notebook back inside his jacket pocket and accepted the glass from her.

"Thanks," she replied, still feeling a little wary.

"But it doesn't really say a lot about you, does it?"

She found the comment curious. On the contrary, she thought the way she'd furnished the place said a lot about her. True, there weren't a lot of decorations, save a couple of inexpensive paintings of still lifes, her collection of candlesticks and a few magazines. But the things that were there said a lot about her. And the absence of other things said even more.

"You don't think it suits me?" she asked. "Why not?"

He lifted one shoulder and let it drop. "It suits you fine," he said. "It just doesn't reveal much about you. There are no photographs of your family or friends. No plants. No books. No music. Nothing that really says anything about who you are. What you are. Where you came from. Where you've been." He smiled again, but there was something about his expression that made it look a little…off. "I mean, you might as well have just appeared in Northaven out of nowhere."

Rosie's stomach clenched tight as he concluded his remarks. He couldn't possibly be saying what he seemed to be saying. There was no way he could know that, for all intents and purposes, she *had* just appeared in Northaven out of nowhere. Because before she came to Northaven, she *hadn't* been Rosie Bliss. Not by name, not by number. Not even by personality, truth be told. Not that she was going to reveal any of that to him. Or anyone else.

"I usually check books out from the library," she said, choosing her words—and her expression—carefully. "The new Maguire Browsing Collection is excellent, by the way," she added to deliberately goad him. She knew as well as everyone else in town how it had come about. "And what few books I do have I keep in the bedroom. Most of my music I download onto my iPod. As for photographs…" She shrugged. "I'm not very photogenic."

He laughed at that, for the first time sounding—seeming—genuine. "Now that I find hard to believe," he told her.

"No, really," she assured him. "I don't like being photographed." Which was most definitely the truth. What she didn't tell him was that her reason for feeling that way was because the last time she'd been photographed, it had nearly cost her her life.

"What about the rest of your family?" he asked. "Your friends? I mean, I know you said you and your mother don't get along, but there must be other people you care about. People who care about you in return."

Was he fishing? she wondered. Trying to find out if she had a boyfriend or ex hanging around somewhere? It was exactly the sort of getting-to-know-you information she'd envisioned sharing with him tonight. Hey, she wouldn't mind knowing if he had an ex hanging around herself. So why did she suddenly feel as if he were indulging less in small talk than he was an interrogation?

She pushed the impression away. He was a cop. He probably made ordering a pizza sound like an interrogation. "I don't just not get along with my mother," she told him reluctantly. "I'm actually estranged from her. I haven't seen her for years. I don't have any other family. And I don't really make friends that easily."

In an effort to curb any further questioning—or, rather, questions, she corrected herself—she lifted her wine in a silent toast and then sipped it, hoping that might encourage Sam to taste his wine, too. Thereby giving him something to do with his mouth besides talk. Not that she didn't have at least one other idea of what he could do that would put his mouth to good use....

Oh, hell. She'd been trying to break her record for how long she could go without thinking about stuff like that. She was heartened—some—when she glanced down at her watch to find she had at least managed to do that. Almost six full minutes had passed without her thinking about having sex with Sam.

He lifted his wine for her toast but didn't taste it right away, something that made Rosie wonder if maybe he was indeed going to use his mouth for something else. He did, but not what she'd been hoping he'd use it for. Instead, he began to talk again.

"You haven't seen your mother for years?" he asked.

She supposed that would be interesting to a man who was close enough to his own mother that he bought her flowers for no special reason. "No, I haven't," she told him after only a small hesitation. She was, after all, the one who'd brought it up. The least she could do was not sidestep the subject. But she said nothing more, hoping he'd take the hint that she really didn't want to talk about it.

No such luck.

"Any particular reason?" he asked.

"No," she said. "There are actually lots of particular reasons."

"Mind if I—"

"Yes," she said. "I do. Look, Sam," she quickly added, holding up a hand when she realized he was going to object. "I didn't exactly have an easy time of it when I was young. And before I moved to Northaven, my life was kind of a mess. I learned a lot from my mistakes, and I've done my best since I came here to rebuild. I keep my eye on the future now, and I enjoy the present as much as I can. Frankly, I'd just as soon forget about the past."

Well, that was partly true. Although Rosie didn't think about the past as much as she used to, being involved, however ignorantly, with a vicious criminal wasn't exactly the kind of thing a woman could forget. And as the saying went, those who forgot history were doomed to repeat it. She'd already repeated it once, endangering herself again in Boulder, and it had nearly gotten her killed. She learned from her mistakes better than most people did—possibly because her mistakes were colossal frigging whoppers that most people didn't commit—and she wasn't about to repeat them over and over. So although she didn't dwell on the past, it was never far from her thoughts. She couldn't afford to let it be.

"I'd rather talk about where I am now," she hurried on before Sam could ask her more about it. "Or where I plan to go in the future. Not where I've been."

As vague and unrevealing a description of herself as she'd just given him, what she told Sam was infinitely more than she'd told anyone else in Northaven. And in a weird way, that suddenly made him her closest friend and most intimate confidant. Even more so than having smokin' sex with him would. Because when all was said and done, sharing her body with someone was a lot easier for Rosie than sharing what lay beneath it.

"You know, maybe if you talked about your past, it would take away some of its power," Sam finally said.

She hoped she looked blithe as she replied, "Who says my past holds any power over me?"

"It has the power to keep you from talking about it."

Rosie sipped her wine casually then asked, "Am I going to be billed for this session? 'Cause I for sure don't remember making an appointment with a therapist."

He grinned at that. "Touché," he said. "And trust me, I didn't come here to analyze you."

She was about to ask him what he had come here to do to her, but he quickly started talking again—almost as if he'd known she was going to ask that—saying, "So then tell me more about your present here in Northaven."

Oh, damn, Rosie thought when she realized how badly she'd set herself up. Truth be told, she'd rather not talk about herself at all, past *or* present. Talking about herself in any version would inevitably lead to revelations, however superficial, and she just wasn't ready to reveal that much of herself to Sam.

It suddenly occurred to her that going out with him—going out with anyone—put her in a position she'd rather not be in. That of creating interest in herself. She didn't know why she hadn't thought about that earlier. Probably, she decided, because it would ultimately force her to accept the fact that she might very well have to spend the rest of her life alone. By virtue of having asked Sam out, however, she had put herself in the position of having to talk about herself. And that hadn't been her intention at all.

Then she remembered that when she'd been weighing the pros and cons of asking Sam out, what had tipped the scales was the potential for smokin' sex at the end of the evening. So that explained that. When she'd asked Sam out, Rosie hadn't been thinking about talking at all. So why were they standing here yammering?

Oh, right. Because it was rude in this society to just open the door to a guy, rip off his clothes and mount him. What was up with that, anyway?

Her thoughts must have shown on her face, because suddenly, Sam seemed to be looking at her in a way that made her think the tearing off of clothes and mounting wouldn't be such a social faux pas after all. Evidently forgetting that he'd just asked her a question, he lifted his glass of wine to his mouth, finally, and drained the entire contents in one lengthy series of swallows. Rosie watched his strong throat muscles work over the wine, noted his gusto in consuming it, and couldn't help wondering if he completed other oral pursuits with equal enthusiasm.

"We should probably get going," he said when he lowered the glass again.

Damn. She was thinking they should probably get coming. She hated those matters of semantics.

"All right," she said, finishing what was left of her own wine in a few hasty sips. "Where are we going?" she added when she was done.

His smile then was inscrutable. "It's a surprise."

5

SAM DIDN'T KNOW if Rosie would actually be surprised by their destination, but he sure as hell was. It wasn't the sort of place he ever took women. Hell, he hardly ever came here himself because he was scared to death someone might see him and start making the wrong kind of assumptions about his character. He just hoped Rosie didn't think it was too kinky or weird. And he hoped she wouldn't decide on the spot that she never wanted to see him again for bringing her to a place like this. A place like…a place like…

Sawyer's Soda Shoppe.

His blood chilled at the sight of the red-and-white-striped awning and the curlicued chairs sitting out front. It just wasn't the kind of place a man who valued his testosterone should be visiting. But date destinations were few and far between in Northaven, and this time of evening, Sawyer's wasn't too busy. The fewer people who saw him and Rosie together tonight, the fewer would be talking about it at church tomorrow.

Not that he had a hope in hell of preventing gossip about the two of them, since gossip was right up there with VFW meetings and the Cookbook Collectors Club as a favorite pastime here. But going to Sawyer's when most people were at home having dinner or going to Kathy's Korner Kafé to eat out would postpone the inevitable for a day or two.

It wasn't that Sam really cared about what people would say when they saw him and Rosie together. He'd just been fending off attempts to fix him up with someone's niece or hairdresser or fellow Cookbook Collectors Club member ever since moving here. He was reasonably certain he'd finally convinced the would-be matchmakers of Northaven that he was a confirmed bachelor and would stay that way. He certainly didn't intend to make a habit out of dating Rosie and had only agreed to go out with her tonight because he hadn't been quick enough on the spot to fabricate a reason for turning her down.

Oh, all right, and also because she'd just looked so crestfallen when he'd told her he was busy Friday night. He'd just have to be careful the next time they went out to ensure that—

He bit back a groan. *Next time,* he echoed to himself. Damn. He had to stop thinking like that. Had to stop thinking about Rosie like that. There wouldn't be a next time, he promised himself. There couldn't be. She was the kind of woman who would have expectations in a relationship. Hell, she was the kind of woman who would expect a relationship, period. And Sam didn't do relationships. He wasn't wired for that kind of thing.

The two of them could have a nice time this evening, and with any luck at all, he'd learn a little more about her, enough to enable him to convince both himself and

Ed Dinwiddie that she was just a private person with nothing to hide. At the very least, he would discover enough about her to be able to prove she wasn't peddling drugs on campus.

As he had so often since moving to Northaven, Sam felt as if he were stepping back in time when he entered Sawyer's Soda Shoppe. Either the place hadn't changed a bit since the Sawyer family opened it in the forties, or else it had some majorly convincing retro thing going on. He doubted it was the latter. Nevertheless, the place looked nearly new, from the sparkly linoleum counter and tabletops to the red vinyl booths and stools to the white honeycomb tile flooring. The waitresses were all women Sam's mother's age, dressed in white uniforms with red ruffled aprons and sensible white shoes.

It kind of gave him the creeps, really. But it served its purpose. That purpose being to make sure he didn't find himself completely aroused by Rosie again. And everybody knew there was nothing like stepping into an ice-cream parlor to give a guy a limp dick.

"Wow, this *is* a surprise," Rosie said as she tucked herself into the booth opposite Sam. "I come to Sawyer's for lunch sometimes, but I've never seen you here before."

And after tonight, she never would again, Sam thought. He could feel his testosterone leaching from him already. Though, strangely, as he noted the way Rosie's ample breasts were being pushed out of the top of her dress, his dick suddenly stood tall again, and even went so far as to salute. *Hoo-wah!*

"Well, I figured Kathy's Korner Kafé was going to

be packed on a Saturday night, and we might have a better chance of getting a table here. Plus, Sawyer's has great pie."

Which was true, and which was the one thing that had lured Sam into the ice-cream shop the handful of times he'd been here. Usually, he had Vicky pick him up a slice when she came here to get one for herself. Or, okay, an entire pie when he was having an especially rough day. On Vicky's days off, Sam had to take care of his own pastry addiction. He just didn't stay long enough for the environment to affect his masculinity. Not that he hadn't been tempted a time or two to cup his hands protectively over his manhood while he waited for one of the Sawyer sisters to box up his pie.

He and Rosie had just placed their orders—and God help him, Sam had come *this* close to asking for a chocolate malt, just like Archie and Jughead—when a college-age woman entered and headed straight for the counter. But when she glanced over and saw them seated there, she smiled and lifted a hand in greeting. Since Sam had no idea who she was, he figured Rosie must know her. Sure enough, Rosie lifted a hand in response.

Instead of continuing her path to the counter, the young woman turned and strode to their table. She was wearing the standard university wear of cropped sweater—in this case purple—and baggy khaki cargo pants that rode low on her hips, and her long brown hair was pulled back from her face in a loose braid. She adjusted small, black-framed glasses as she approached, then greeted Rosie by name.

"Hello, Stephanie," Rosie replied. But she began to

fidget in her seat a little, and she didn't meet the other woman's gaze, as if she were uncomfortable about her sudden appearance. In spite of that, she added, "How are you?"

"I'm fine," Stephanie replied. "But I, um…" She glanced at Sam, muttered a quick, "Hey, Chief," then looked back at Rosie. "I need to make an appointment with you. Soon. I need more stuff."

Now Rosie glanced over at Sam, too, and she looked even more anxious than she had before. "That's fine," she said, turning her attention back to Stephanie. "Just call me in the morning, okay? Sam and I are kind of in the middle of something."

Stephanie looked at Sam again, then back at Rosie, then back at Sam. Finally, understanding dawned. *"Ooooohhhhh,"* she said, stringing the word out over several time zones. "I'm sorry. I didn't realize you two were on a date. I didn't mean to interrupt."

But she hesitated before leaving, nibbling her lip a little as she looked back at Rosie. Sam got the impression Rosie wasn't the only one at the table who was uncomfortable.

"Um, what time should I call?" Stephanie asked. "I mean, I *really* need more stuff. Like, *really* soon. I'm getting *really* desperate."

Sam's gut went tight at the young woman's words, because she sounded a lot like she needed the kind of thing Ed Dinwiddie was sure Rosie was providing his students. Immediately, he reminded himself that even junkies weren't stupid enough to try to score drugs in front of a law enforcement officer. Still, Stephanie's words—and her behavior—were a little odd. Odd, too, was how Rosie was acting.

Guilty. There was no other word to describe it.

"I'll be at the store at eight," she told Stephanie, looking anxious. "Call me anytime after that."

"Great," Stephanie said. "I think Brianna needs to get some more, too. I'll let you know."

"Good," Rosie said, sliding another nervous glance at Sam. "I'll look forward to talking to you."

Sam watched Stephanie go, looking for signs of addiction. But she seemed perfectly fine as she made her way to the counter. No weaving in her walking, no jitters. Her eyes had been clear when she spoke to Rosie, and her words hadn't been the least slurred. No indication of confusion or disorientation. She looked like a healthy college kid picking up carryout at Sawyer's. And the bag she walked out with was only big enough for a small meal. No munchies, then.

Nevertheless, Sam looked at Rosie and smiled. "Stuff?" he said, hoping his voice sounded light and teasing. "What kind of stuff? You peddling something out of your shop I should know about, Ms. Bliss?"

Rosie chuckled in reply, but it was unmistakably forced. She sounded more nervous now than she had talking to Stephanie, and whatever had tightened Sam's gut a moment ago now went icy cold. It turned downright Arctic when she only looked at him for a moment without replying, as if she were scouring her brain for some way to answer the question that would skirt the truth.

Finally, "Potpourri," she said. "Stephanie wants more potpourri."

"Potpourri," Sam echoed dubiously.

Rosie nodded quickly, but wouldn't meet his gaze. Instead, she worried a small scar on the table with her finger. "Yeah, potpourri. The girls like to have it in their dorms to keep the rooms from smelling stale. I do a different blend for each one of them."

"Ah. Interesting that Stephanie didn't call it potpourri."

"Well, that's one of those words that intimidates a lot of people," Rosie said by way of an explanation.

"Mmm," Sam replied.

When Rosie looked up again, two spots of pink had appeared on her cheeks. She was blushing, Sam marveled. He couldn't remember the last time he'd seen a woman blush. But of course she would blush, he told himself. Nice women always blushed when they were caught in a fib. And Rosie was one of the nicest of all.

Even if she *was* fibbing about the potpourri. That much Sam knew. He wasn't sure what kind of *stuff* Rosie was supplying the women at Northaven College, but it wasn't that. And the fact that she could feel so muddled about being dishonest intrigued Sam more than he should have let it. Especially since he wasn't intrigued the way a cop would be intrigued. He was intrigued the way a man would be. And that way lay madness. Not to mention an ethics violation.

"So what brought you to Northaven from Boston?" Rosie asked in an obvious effort to change the subject.

Not that Sam minded. For now. He just wished she'd changed it to something else. Even a discussion of the mating habits of giant squids would be preferable to him talking about himself.

"Oldest story in the world," he said. "Urban cop becomes disenchanted with the ugliness of the big city so he goes where the air is clean and the people don't brutalize each other."

He'd tried to make the comment sound offhand and carefree, but feared it came out sounding bitter and angry instead. Doubtless because that was how he always felt whenever he thought about his job in Boston, particularly the last case that had finally pushed him over the edge. He supposed there was no way to make light what had been so dark. No way to inject indifference into what had been so awful. Even with more than a year between him and that last case, his gut still burned to think about it.

"Was there anything in particular about the urban ugliness that made you leave it all behind?" Rosie asked. "I mean, that's a pretty major change, Boston to Northaven."

He started to echo her reply of a little while ago, wanted to tell her that no, it was a lot of particular things that did it. Instead, he heard himself say, "A pimp beat one of his hookers to death. My partner and I knew her fairly well."

Rosie's brows arrowed downward in what he could see was genuine shock and concern. "I'm sorry, Sam."

"She was only fourteen."

Rosie's mouth dropped open at that.

Helpless to stop himself, Sam suddenly began pouring out the story, as if it were a tipping vat of poison he couldn't begin to right. "Roni was the girl's name. She was a good kid—a nice kid—who'd had some lousy breaks. Started using when she was still in elementary school. Ran away from home when she was twelve. Got into hooking not long after that. My partner and I were trying to get her into a program, trying to get her off the streets. We'd found a place for her and had finally talked her into leaving her pimp. We told her to just get in the car and we'd take her to a safe place, supply her with everything she'd need, but she wanted to do the right thing and tell the son of a bitch she was quitting. Said she'd meet us at the address later. But she never showed. Homicide guys found her body that night in a Roxbury alley."

Sam wanted to slap a hand over his mouth to make himself shut the hell up. He hadn't told anyone in North-aven about Roni. He hadn't even allowed himself to think about the case—the girl—since moving here. He was supposed to be on a date, for chrissakes, and this wasn't exactly the kind of lighthearted banter two people indulged in during their first dinner together—or any dinner together, for that matter. He had no idea what made him spill his guts to Rosie that way. And he wished like hell he could take back every word.

Especially when he looked up at her again to see that her eyes were damp with tears. God, he was such a jerk. He hadn't meant to make her cry.

"I'm sorry," he quickly apologized. "I shouldn't have told you all that. It's not the kind of thing you're used to talking about, and it's way too ugly for dinner conversation. I never—"

"Sam, it's okay," she interrupted him.

Then she did the strangest thing. She inched her fingers across the table and, after just a tiny hesitation, covered his hand with hers. Even stranger was the fact that Sam let her do it. He didn't pull his hand out from under hers the way he would have, had someone else touched him that way. It was a comforting touch, and he didn't like it when people tried to comfort him. He wasn't a comfortable person. And he sure as hell didn't deserve comfort. Not when there were so many other people out there who needed it and had earned it more but were denied it daily. Not when he was supposed to be one of the people making the world a more comfortable place and instead let little girls get killed.

But he didn't remove his hand from beneath Rosie's. In fact, he turned it over, so that his palm was nestled against hers. Her skin was warm against his, soft, and as he touched her wrist with his middle finger, he felt her pulse thrumming against his fingertip. When he closed his fingers over her hand, that pulse quickened, thumping faster and harder on his flesh. Rosie curled her fingers closed, too, clasping his hand in hers.

She said nothing, only blinked and spilled a single fat tear onto her cheek that she hastily swiped away with the back of her other hand. And somehow, Sam got the feeling she understood perfectly what he'd been feeling for a long, long time.

"Don't apologize," she told him. "Don't ever apologize for being shocked by something horrifying. Don't apologize for having strong feelings. And don't apologize for wanting to share them. It just shows how human you are."

"But this isn't the time—"

"It's the perfect time," she told him, braving a small smile. "We're getting to know each other, aren't we? And you just told me a lot about yourself."

He muttered a derisive sound. "Yeah, that I have no idea how to show a woman a good time."

"No," she immediately denied. "That you're one of a dying breed. A decent guy." She looked down at their joined hands and moved her fingers so that they were interwoven more snugly with his. And then she smiled again. A sweet, kind, gentle smile. The sort of smile he didn't deserve. The sort of smile he nonetheless craved.

And just like that, he felt his spirits lifting and his head returning to where it needed to be. With Rosie Bliss. In a Norman Rockwell setting. Which somehow, suddenly, didn't feel quite as threatening to Sam's masculinity as it had before. In fact, the way Rosie was looking at him now…

Well. His masculinity might not ever be the same…

BY THE TIME they made it back to Rosie's apartment, it was after midnight, and Rosie was marveling at what a good time she and Sam had had together. After sandwiches at Sawyer's, they'd seen the movie playing at the Palace Theatre, then strolled back to Rosie's place through the park discussing the finer points of the film. Sam was a much bigger movie buff than she, and he'd suggested a number of cinematic masterpieces she absolutely had to see, and, hey, since he had so many of them on DVD, he'd just have to bring some over to her place next time so they could enjoy some private viewings.

She couldn't believe she'd initially feared their date would be a disaster. They'd just been so awkward together at first. Good God, she'd even suspected him of snooping in her desk. Their conversation had been stilted all the way to Sawyer's, and everything had felt so weird. But somewhere along the way, everything had evened out, and the two of them had ended up talking about everything.

Except, she hadn't been able to help noticing, each other.

Of course, she knew why they hadn't talked about her. But even if she hadn't talked about herself tonight, she'd discovered something very important about herself. Because at one point, when she'd been sidestepping one of Sam's many questions about her past—a subject he just hadn't quite been able to let go—she'd found herself thinking she might tell him about some of her past experiences someday, just not today. Which meant she'd already begun to think in terms of future dates—or something—with Sam.

Not that thinking about future dates with Sam was so earth-shattering, since she'd found herself thinking about that—or, at least, fantasizing about it—ever since meeting him. It was the *or something* that cropped up that really threw her. Even on the outside chance that she someday ended up in a—oh, hell, she might as well just say it, at least to herself—a *relationship* with someone, Rosie had just never thought she'd ever have it in her to open up to that person and tell him everything about her past and where and who she'd been once upon a time. And although she couldn't see herself telling Sam about everything, she found herself thinking that maybe, someday, there was a vague possibility she might reveal a little. Because she was beginning to think he was the kind of guy who wouldn't be put off by her past.

Even more significant, he was starting to seem like the kind of guy who might care for her in spite of it.

She knew she was getting *waaaaaaay* ahead of herself with that kind of thinking, so as she turned the key in the lock of her front door, she pushed all thoughts of such things away. Of course, doing that left her with some troubling thoughts instead, not the least of which was the realization that she had come to the end of her date with Sam, and it had been so long since she'd been on a date with a guy that she wasn't sure what she should do.

So as she pushed the door open, she turned around and asked, "Do you want to come in for another glass of wine? I hate opening a bottle and not finishing it."

"You don't think you'll finish it yourself?" he asked, clearly conflicted about the invitation.

She shook her head. "I hate to drink alone." To herself, she added, *Among other things.*

For a minute, she thought he was going to decline. Then he lifted a shoulder and let it drop. "Well, I'd hate for it to go to waste."

So would Rosie. Oh, wait. He was probably talking about the wine, wasn't he?

She shrugged off her sweater and draped it over the chair as she made her way to the kitchen. This time Sam did follow her, and even went so far as to claim the bottle of wine from the counter where Rosie had left it while she went to retrieve two fresh glasses. As she opened the cabinet, she noticed the red light on her answering machine flashing. One, two, three times quickly, then a pause. Three calls. Probably at least one of them from Stephanie. Once those girls ran out of tea, they were always so desperate to reorder.

Sam must have noticed the flashing light, too, because as he came to a stop behind her, he said, "Looks like you've got a few messages."

"I'll play them tomorrow."

"You can play them now, if you want. I don't mind."

She shook her head. Bad enough he'd been privy to her exchange with Stephanie earlier. She just hoped he bought the potpourri explanation. "It's too late to call anyone back tonight," she told him. "It will wait."

The only clean wine glasses were on the top shelf of the cabinet, so Rosie pushed herself up on tiptoe to try and grab them. Unfortunately, they were just beyond her reach, and no amount of stretching would push her fingers any closer.

"Here, let me," Sam offered as he set the wine on the counter. "I can get them."

But he didn't wait for her to move out of the way and stepped up behind her, his entire body pressing into hers, from his thighs to the arm he extended parallel to hers, over their heads. He halted, however, before his fingers made contact with the glasses, and Rosie wondered if it was because he felt the same shudder of heat she felt the moment the two of them connected in all the places they did.

Neither moved for a moment, only stood motionless

with their bodies pressed together as if each was waiting
to see what the other would do. And in that moment, fire
sparked in Rosie's belly and slowly seeped to every inch
of her body. Sam's heat and scent surrounded her, en-
veloped her, mingled with her own. His hand beside hers
was twice the size of her own, rough where hers was
smooth, dark where hers was fair, hard where hers was
soft. And all she could do was wonder how his long,
strong fingers would feel raking over her tender flesh.

Her pulse leaped at the thought, and she was carried
back to the morning in her shop, when he'd stood so
close, smelled so erotic, looked so aroused, and made
her so unbearably hot. And suddenly, Rosie knew a
need so fierce, so fundamental and so profound that she
feared she would spontaneously combust. It had simply
been too long since she'd been this attracted to a man,
too long since she'd been touched by a man, too long
since she'd made love with a man.

Rosie had always loved sex. Had reveled in it. Had
rejoiced in it. She loved the way her body fit so well with
a man's, loved the brawn and sinew and power in the
male body. She loved looking at the elegant lines of the
naked male form, loved the dips and swells of muscle
and flesh. She'd missed men. She'd missed sex. And the
idea of having both tonight was simply more than she
could tolerate. She wanted Sam. Needed Sam. And she
would have given anything—anything—in that moment
to have him.

She was battling the urge to turn around and cover
his mouth with hers in a way that would convince him
to stay very late tonight, when she instead felt his other

arm slip slowly around her waist. Her sigh was a mixture of both anticipation and satisfaction, and as she leaned back into him, she felt him stir to life against her bottom. He was even warmer now, his presence behind her more palpable, his scent musky and dark. Ah, yes. The male animal. It was all coming back to her now.

"I, ah…" he began, his voice a soft murmur by her ear, "I guess I should've, um, let you move out of the way first, huh?"

She grinned. Oh, she wasn't so sure about that….

"No," she replied as quietly as he, "this is just fine." She moved her hand to cover his, which he'd splayed open over her torso, pushing her fingers between his. "More than fine," she added. "It feels good. You feel good, Sam." *Too good,* she wanted to add.

When he didn't respond to her assertion, she worried that saying even that much might have been too much. But then he slid his other arm around her waist, too, and pulled her more intimately against him. Rosie reached behind herself to thread her fingers through his hair, a position that left her chest thrusting forward. Sam wasn't stupid—he took advantage, as she'd hoped he would, moving one hand to cradle the lower swell of her breast in the deep V of his thumb and forefinger. He strummed the fingers of his other hand first up, then down along her rib cage, taking Rosie's hand along for the ride. Up over her belly he journeyed, then down again, to her thigh, her hip, and finally, between her legs. Her dress hindered him from doing more than pushing his long fingers against the front of her, but he pushed hard as he stroked her, up and down, again and again.

Rosie moaned softly at the delicious friction, so exquisite was his touch. Sam groaned in response, ducking his head into her neck, rubbing his open mouth along the sensitive column of her throat. He pulled her body back toward him even more, covering her breast now over the fabric of her dress with one big hand. He squeezed her sensitive flesh hard, drawing another soft cry from within her, and Rosie thrust her chest forward in silent encouragement that he do it again. As he did, his other hand pushed harder against her damp center, this time making her hiss her delight. She reached up to cover the hand he had clasped on her breast, and began to guide it in ever-increasing circles.

As they massaged her breast together, Sam moved the hand between her legs to her hip, bunching the fabric of her dress in his fist to jerk it up over her thighs and around her waist. Rosie pushed her bottom against him again, and his cock surged harder against her. When he began to skim his hand back down, he brushed his fingers over her ass, groaning when he realized it was bared to his touch, thanks to the thong. Instead of returning to her damp core, Sam opened his hand over her naked flesh and mimicked the actions of his other hand, squeezing her ass and her breast in perfect time. So Rosie moved her own hand between her legs, stroking herself through the damp fabric of her panties, again and again and again.

But even that wasn't enough. She needed Sam there with her. So she circled her fingers around his wrist and drew his hand from her breast downward, shepherding it into her panties. He needed no further instruction or encouragement. Dipping his hand beneath the elastic, he furrowed his fingers deep into her wet flesh, catching the sensitive bud of her clitoris to roll it gently between his thumb and forefinger, then dipping his long middle finger into her slick canal. Rosie parted her legs to facilitate his maneuvers, and he cupped her sex fully in his palm, rubbing slowly, methodically, thoroughly.

When she thrust her hips forward, he pushed his finger inside her again, deeper this time. When Rosie murmured the word *Yes,* he withdrew his finger and drilled her again, then a second time, then a third, then more times than she could count. In and out he thrust his finger, sliding it over the sensitive folds of her flesh every time he withdrew. Rosie whispered more words, frantic words, words like *faster* and *deeper* and *harder* and *again,* until finally her orgasm rocked her. Her entire body went rigid as she came, then she relaxed and slumped back against Sam, panting hard.

She wasn't sure how long they stood that way, simply enjoying the sensations of touching so intimately and being so intimately touched, but eventually, Sam pulled away from her and gently pushed her dress back into place. Rosie thought at first it was because he was going to suggest they retreat to her bedroom, but when she turned around to smile at him, her languid happiness evaporated. Instead of looking like a man who'd just enjoyed a very nice sexual encounter, he looked like a man who'd been told he only had two weeks to live.

"What?" she said, dread uncoiling in her stomach. "What's wrong?"

He didn't reply at first, but his expression faltered,

to the point where she thought maybe she was only imagining his grim reaction. For one brief moment, he looked as though he did indeed intend to sweep her up into his arms and carry her off to her room where he could ravish her more thoroughly than Rhett had Scarlett. His eyes fairly glowed with his desire—with his passion, with his need—and his lips parted, as if he intended to give her a long, leisurely lick.

Then the shutters fell back into place, and he said, "I'm sorry, Rosie. That shouldn't have happened."

The dread in her belly seeped into her chest. "Why not?"

He looked at her then as if she should already know the answer to the question. "Why not?" he echoed.

She nodded. "Why not? I like you, you like me. I was turned-on, you were turned-on. Hell, we're both still turned-on. We both obviously want each other. We're consenting adults in the privacy of my own home. Why shouldn't that have happened? For that matter, why shouldn't *more* happen?" She lifted a hand to his hair and pushed a stray lock from his forehead. "I want to make love with you, Sam. Tonight. Here. Now. What could there possibly be to stop us?"

He seemed stumped for a moment—stumped for an answer anyway, since the rest of him was anything *but* stumped, his cock having pushed harder against her thigh with every word she spoke. Then he said, "Because we barely know each other."

Rosie actually laughed at that. Once. Nervously. But laughed nonetheless. "I know you better than I know anyone in Northaven," she told him. "Maybe we didn't talk too much about ourselves tonight, Sam, but…" Taking a chance, she pushed herself up on tiptoe and touched her lips to his—quickly, chastely—then went down on her feet again. "But we learned a lot about each other," she assured him.

She lifted her hand toward his face again, but where she feared he might try to jerk his head out of her reach, instead, he leaned into her touch—almost imperceptibly, but he did meet her halfway.

"We know each other better than you think," she said softly.

"We still shouldn't be doing this," he told her, his eyes looking haunted for some reason.

"Why not?" she asked again. And then it hit her. What she'd been thinking about earlier. About any exes he might have in the world. Maybe he didn't have an ex at all. Maybe he was still in love with someone somewhere.

But why should that matter? Rosie asked herself. She didn't want a long-term thing with Sam. She just wanted to have a good time for a little while. Enjoy some smokin' sex with a smokin' sexy man. Relieve the sexual tension she felt every time she was within fifty feet of him. She wanted to give her Xtacy 2000 a little rest. Enjoy some Xtacy Sam Maguire instead. She didn't want him to fall in love with her any more than she wanted to fall in love with him.

But she couldn't quite stop the question from coming. "Is there someone else?"

Immediately, she wanted to kick herself for asking. Not because she didn't want to hear the answer, but because the question had sounded so possessive. By asking if there was someone else, Rosie had just indicated she wanted to be someone. Someone special. Someone to whom Sam was committed. And nothing could be further from the truth.

"I mean…" she tried to backpedal. Unfortunately, she wasn't sure what she meant.

"It's not that," Sam said.

"Then what?" she asked. And she told herself to ignore the thread of relief that wound through her at hearing him say there was no one else. That didn't matter. It didn't.

"I'm just not sure it's a good idea," he said.

She leaned up to kiss him again, this time slanting her mouth over his for a longer, more thorough taste. For a second, he didn't kiss her back, and Rosie knew a disappointment so acute, she wasn't sure she'd be able to handle it. Then he was roping his arms around her again and bending his head over hers, taking full control of the embrace. Very, *very* willingly, Rosie surrendered to him.

For a while, they only kissed, long, deep, passionate kisses she felt to the very depths of her soul. Then Rosie inched her hand down his chest, to the belt fastened at his waist, and hastily jerked it free. He seemed about to object, so she kissed him more deeply, thrusting her tongue into his mouth as she unbuttoned his fly and tugged the zipper down. His cock pushed against her hand the moment she tucked her fingers inside, and she stroked him, once, twice, three times, four, until he was hard as a rock in her grip.

And then she dropped to her knees in front of him. He uttered a wild sound as she sucked him into her mouth, curving the fingers of one hand over the back of her head and pushing her hair back with the other so that he could better see what she was doing. She pushed her head forward, pulling as much of him into her mouth as she could, pushing him to the very back of her throat. He tasted earthy and musky and male, and she took her time to enjoy him. Circling his cock with sure fingers, she held him still while she traced lazy lines with the tip of her tongue, first around the plump head, then down the length of him and back up again. She nibbled his flesh and nipped him with her teeth, loving the way his breath hissed out of his mouth when she did. Then she covered him again, sucking him deep, until he moaned his pleasure again.

In and out of her mouth Rosie moved him, until she knew he was close to coming. Then she stood and covered his mouth with hers again, thrusting her tongue inside his, hoping he enjoyed the taste of himself on her tongue as much as she did. He returned her kiss with the fierceness of a man possessed, tangling his fingers in her hair and tugging on the long tresses until her head was tipped back so that he could plunder her mouth at will. Then she felt his fingers at the top of her zipper, and slowly, slowly, oh…so…slowly, Sam began to tug it down, down, down.

She felt the cool kiss of air on her back as the garment fell open, then he pushed it gently down over her shoulders so that he could skim his lips over the tender flesh that was revealed. Rosie shimmied out of the garment until it was pooled around her ankles, then circled his neck with both arms to thread her fingers through his hair. It was so silky, so soft. She'd forgotten how erotic a man's hair could feel, the sensual way it curled around her fingers, as if wanting to be trapped there forever.

Sam took his kisses lower then, to the divot at the base of her throat, her collarbone, her breastbone, then to the deep crevice of her cleavage. He ran his tongue over the swells of breast spilling out of the top of her bra, then deftly unhooked the garment and let it fall to the floor beside her dress. And then his hands were on her breasts, naked flesh on naked flesh, and the sensation shooting through her was glorious.

As he lifted his head to kiss her again, he palmed her breasts zealously, once, twice, three times, four, then caught her nipples between the thumb and forefinger of each hand, rolling them gently before opening his hands over her again. One hand skimmed lower this time, though, between their bodies, following the same path he had traveled before, into her panties to weave through the soft hair between her legs. Then lower still, to the hot, wet flesh that demanded his touch.

Rosie took a step to the side to spread her legs wider and give him better access. So he scooped his hand deeper, sliding one long finger inside her again. She gasped at the depth and quickness of his entry this time, bucking her hips forward now to force him deeper still. He drew a slow, thorough circle inside her, then withdrew his finger to push it inside her again. Over and over he thrust into and out of her, Rosie panting and jerking with every new foray until waves of pleasure began to rock her.

His touch was incredible. His fingers felt so much better inside her than her own….

Her second orgasm came more quickly than the first, but the ripples of pleasure took their time to ebb. She wasn't close to being satisfied, however. Not that that was a problem, she knew. She and Sam were just getting started. Why, he wasn't even undressed yet, a condition she intended to rectify right away.

He looked truly and profoundly aroused now, all traces of his earlier confusion and reluctance gone. His gaze settled on hers for just a moment, then dropped lower, to her naked breasts. Without a word, he lifted one in his hand and bent forward, then gave the nipple a light little lick with his tongue. That was followed by another, slightly longer lick, then another that was longer still. Rosie tangled the fingers of both hands in his hair now, closing her eyes when he covered the top of her breast with his mouth and sucked as much of her as he could inside.

As he squeezed and sucked her breast, he moved his other hand to her bottom, kneading the sensitive flesh with much enthusiasm. Never in her life had Rosie felt more aroused, standing nearly naked in her kitchen with a fully clothed man as he ravished her from the front and back both. She remembered she'd planned to undress him. But now she began to see some merit to his being clothed.

It just felt so naughty, so politically incorrect. She liked the feeling of vulnerability her current state brought, because, somehow, ironically, it made her feel so powerful, too. As helpless as she was to resist Sam and the things he was doing to her, she knew she had the same effect on him. He was under her control as much as she was his at the moment. He could no more resist her than she could him. And that only made her want him more.

For long minutes, he focused on her breasts, moving from one to the other as he tried to consume each in turn. Then he straightened, and covered her mouth with his. As he kissed her, rolling his tongue deep into her mouth, he began to slowly move backward, bringing Rosie with him until he reached a chair pushed back against the wall. He hooked his thumbs into the waistband of her panties and pushed them down, then dropped his own trousers and folded himself into the chair. Rosie hooked a leg over him and fell into his lap, straddling him. She roped her arms around his neck, threaded her fingers through his hair again, then leaned in to kiss him this time, capturing his tongue and sucking hard. She felt his hands open over her bare back, then move lower, cupping the curves of her ass and squeezing hard.

Impatient to touch him, too, she feverishly began to unbutton his shirt, pushing it and his jacket both from his shoulders when she was done. As they warred for possession of the kiss, Sam helped her jerk his arms out of the sleeves and cast the clothing aside, until finally, her naked skin could connect with his.

The sensation of hot flesh rubbing against hot flesh was almost more than she could bear. It had been so long. Too long. Too long since she'd had sex with a living breathing creature who could touch her and fill her the way she needed to be touched and filled.

"Now, Sam," she gasped against his mouth. "I need to feel you inside me now."

Without awaiting a response, she pushed herself up

on tiptoe, gripping Sam's cock in sure fingers. Then she guided him beneath her and came back down on top of him, filling herself with the sheer size and strength of him. He stretched and filled her, until she wasn't sure where she ended and he began. Then he cupped her ass in both hands and lifted her up, pulling her back down even harder.

Rosie took the hint and began moving herself with him, and within minutes, together, they came with a shattering orgasm. Never in her life had Rosie come that quickly, that completely, with a man. And all she could think about was doing it again. Immediately.

"I think we need to take this party to the bedroom," she said breathlessly. "It could be a while before we've had enough."

His dark eyes went darker still at the suggestion. "Do you know how incredibly sexy you are?" he asked.

She grinned. "Yeah. I can tell by the sounds you make when I have you in my mouth."

He made another one of those sounds in response to her assertion, then said, "Just wait till I get you in mine."

This time it was Rosie's turn to utter such a sound. She felt a little shaky as she stood, but when she extended a hand to Sam and he took it, she felt a little steadier. She told herself she should feel weird, standing naked in her kitchen with a man who was nearly naked himself. Instead, she felt profoundly aroused. Hand in hand, they strode to her bedroom, pausing every few steps to entwine themselves together for some deep-throated kissing. When they finally arrived in Rosie's room, she turned down the bed while Sam finished undressing. Then she crawled onto the bed, deliberately giving him a good view of her ass, turning at the center of the mattress to face him as she tucked her legs beneath her.

She caught her breath at the sight of him naked. Dark hair spanned his chest and torso, arrowing down to nest over his powerful cock. He was just so male, so potent, so incredibly masculine. And she was going to have sex with him. All night long, she hoped. Because she already knew one time with Sam wasn't going to be enough. One night with Sam wasn't going to be enough, either, quite frankly. But she wouldn't think about that right now, she told herself. Right now, she would only think about…

"Right now," she told him. "I want you right now."

He joined her on the bed, cupping a hand behind her nape as he kissed her and laid her down alongside him. At first he only kissed her. Kissed her and stroked his hand along the side of her body, from her shoulder to her waist to her hip to her thigh and back again. Then he rolled onto his own back and pulled her atop him to kiss her some more. Eventually, though, he urged her up again, cupping both hands on her hips to guide her astride him. Slowly, he pushed her forward, toward his head, until her knees were snuggled against ribs. Then he cupped her ass with both hands and pushed her forward even more. With one final push, he brought her to the place where he wanted her. Lifting his head from the pillow he dipped it between her legs and began to tongue her sensitive flesh.

Rosie's eyes fluttered closed as he licked her, and she

reached for the headboard, clutching it tighter with every stroke of his tongue. She felt his hands drift from her hips to her ass, then his fingers delving into the tender line bisecting it. As he urged her forward and savored her wet flesh with his mouth, darting his tongue into her slick canal, he gently pushed a finger down to the first knuckle into her behind. She gasped in surprise at the double penetration, then sighed, feeling very, *very* aroused.

Sam took his time eating her, driving her mad with the dual pleasuring of his finger and his tongue. But before she lost herself in another orgasm, he withdrew from her, pushing her backward down his body until she felt his hard cock pressing against her. Rising up on her knees, she began to lower herself onto him. But he bucked his hips up to enter her more quickly, more thoroughly, and she gasped with pleasure at the intensity of his penetration. As big as he was, he filled her perfectly, his size generating a delicious friction as he thrust in and out of her. Rosie joined him, pushing herself up and down on her knees in a rapid rhythm that mimicked his own.

Just as she felt her orgasm swelling inside her, Sam gripped her hips again and lifted her off of him, turning both their bodies so that Rosie was on her back and he was lying atop her, his arms braced on the mattress on each side of her head, his rough chest abrading her own, his flat torso pressing into hers.

"I want to watch you up close while you come," he whispered roughly.

And she very nearly did right then.

Everything after that was a swirl of pleasure, sensation and delight. Rosie cupped her hands behind Sam's hot neck as he thrust deep and hard inside her. With one final heave, he came, just as a shot of white heat exploded from her center to sear her every extremity. In that moment, Rosie knew a moment of panic. Because she realized then that not only would one night with Sam never be enough…

A lifetime with him wouldn't be enough, either.

6

HOURS AFTER RETURNING to Rosie's apartment, Sam lay beside her in her bed feeling more exhausted than he'd ever felt in his life. But it was a pleasant kind of lethargy that made his entire body relax. He couldn't remember the last time he'd felt this way. Maybe he never had. He felt…content. Easy. Almost euphoric. As if every ounce of tension he'd ever absorbed had been wrung from his body. As if all the ugliness he'd witnessed in the world had been squeezed from his heart. As if all the poison and deceit and malice that had slithered under his skin over the years had been chased away forever.

He felt good. Nice. He felt very good. Very nice. He wanted to feel this way forev—

Oh, no, he stopped himself before the thought could fully form in his brain. No, no, no, no, no. He couldn't feel this way forever. He wasn't supposed to feel this way at all. He didn't deserve to feel good. He didn't deserve to feel nice. He hadn't earned it. Had, in fact, sacrificed the right to both when he'd failed so egregiously to do his job serving and protecting people like Roni. Now Sam had to do whatever he could to make sure goodness and niceness survived in the world. But he wasn't allowed to participate in them. There would be no good for him. No nice. Not now. Not ever.

When he turned to look at Rosie, who lay on her side looking back at him, his panic multiplied. She was the very opposite of what he was entitled to, the opposite of what he deserved. She was so beautiful. So sensual. So incredibly, unspeakably fine. Her hair was a riot of dark auburn cascading over her forehead and shoulders, and her eyes were all dreamy and soft. Her skin was pink from the aftermath of their passion, darker in the places where he'd scruffed her with his rough beard. And although he knew it was politically incorrect to feel this way—not to mention he had no right to feel it—a thrill of masculine delight wound through him as he realized he'd marked her, however temporarily, as his.

Temporarily, he repeated to himself, heartening some. Maybe it would be okay to feel this way for just a little while. Just tonight. It wasn't as though he and Rosie were destined to be together forever. They'd just sort of lost control this evening and succumbed to a normal human urge. It had been a while since Sam had enjoyed a sexual encounter with someone other than, well, himself, and he knew Rosie hadn't dated anyone but Mr. Xtacy 2000 for some time now. The human sex drive was a powerful thing, second only to a person's will to survive. And there had been times in his life when Sam had been certain his survival depended on having a sexual encounter. He and Rosie were both very sexual creatures. And neither had been able to resist the temptation.

Once.

Because it wouldn't happen again, he vowed. He couldn't let it happen again. Hell, even without his being undeserving, he still wasn't sure about Rosie's origins or identity before coming to Northaven. He still wasn't convinced she was involved in any wrongdoing. But he wasn't sure she was entirely on the up-and-up, either. Even after he did uncover the truth about her—which he most certainly would do—regardless of what that truth held, Sam had to make sure he steered clear of any more sexual escapades with her. There were just too many ways that being with her could and would be wrong.

"What are you thinking about?" she asked, her voice as dreamy and soft as the rest of her.

Great. That was the last question any man wanted to hear from a woman, but especially not right after having sex with her. Add to it the fact that what he'd been thinking about was how he intended to never have sex with her again, and he *really* didn't want to reply.

So he hedged, "I'm thinking about how incredible that was. How incredible you are. Rosie, I don't think I've ever had better sex in my entire life than I had tonight." And he was surprised to realize he'd just told her the absolute truth.

Though he probably should have prettied up the sentiment before voicing it. Even though he'd meant it as a compliment, she'd probably take it wrong and conclude that sex was more important to him than anything else. And although that might have been true another time—with other women—this time it wasn't. The sex had indeed been great. But Rosie had been better. And not just in a sexual way.

Which was yet another reason why, from here on out, Sam had to keep his distance from her.

But before he could backtrack and try to explain what he meant, she started chuckling, sounding genuinely pleased by what he'd told her. "Good," she said. "Because it was incredible for me, too. I don't think I've ever had the earth move quite that way before, either."

He smiled at that, unable to prevent the masculine pride that swelled his chest. Among other things. Until he remembered he shouldn't be feeling anything except strong in his convictions that something like this would never happen again.

Dammit. Okay, so maybe one more time with Rosie wouldn't hurt, he told himself. As long as he promised himself it wouldn't happen anymore *after* that…

He pushed the thought away. But he still couldn't quite keep himself from asking, "So, on the Richter scale of sex, what number would you say it was?"

She narrowed her eyes in thought. "I don't know. What number does the Richter scale of sex go up to?"

"I think eight is considered pretty devastating."

She nodded. "Okay. In that case, I'd have to say you caused a quake of about seven hundred and forty-two."

He arched his brows at that. "Wow."

"Yeah," she said, grinning. "Wow."

She studied him for a moment more in silence, looking thoughtful enough that he didn't say anything, because he wanted to know what she was thinking about, too. Which was yet another example of how different sex with Rosie had been from sex with other women. Sam didn't usually care what women were thinking about after he had sex with them. He was too busy putting on his pants and making excuses for why he had to leave.

Definitely had to make this the last—and only—time with Rosie. Probably.

"You know," she finally said, "it occurs to me that this could be a very mutually beneficial arrangement."

This time Sam was the one to narrow his eyes. "What do you mean?"

She moved her hand to his chest to draw idle circles on his warm flesh, and even that small gesture made his cock stir between his legs.

"I mean," she said, "that there's obviously something going on between us, some powerful, physical, *very* sexual thing, as evidenced by the way we both sort of lost control tonight."

Sam couldn't deny it, so he didn't. "Yeah. So?"

The hand tracing lines on his chest flattened over his heart, and he felt his cock rise higher.

"So," she began again, "I get the feeling that before tonight, it had been a while since you've had sex."

It had been longer than he cared to think about. And the last few times he'd had sex, it had been with women who were convenient and little else. It hadn't been because he'd been especially attracted to them. So the sex, although satisfying, hadn't been anything spectacular. Certainly it had been nothing like the way it had been with Rosie tonight.

Which was number five on *Late Night*'s Top Ten Reasons Why Sam Maguire Has to Get the Hell Outta Rosie Bliss's Bed, he thought.

"Yeah, it had been a while for me," he told her. "Why?"

The hand splayed open over his heart skimmed down his torso, the fingers brushing lightly over the hair that darkened his lower abdomen. By now, his cock was standing straight again, a clear indication that it begged to differ with Sam's edict that this had to be the one-and-only time with Rosie.

"Because before tonight," she continued, "it had been a while for me, too. And I also get the feeling," she added, "that sex is very important to you."

Uh, yeah, Sam thought. Who didn't think sex was important?

"I mean *really* important," Rosie added, as if she'd read his mind. "Even more important than most people—most men, even—think it is."

He nodded at that. "I've always had a pretty healthy libido, yeah."

"Me, too," she told him frankly. "One that no other man has been able to satisfy the way you did tonight."

Sam grinned in spite of the conflicting emotions plaguing him. He couldn't help himself. "Excuse me, won't you, while I pause for a moment of smugness."

She laughed again, and he decided he liked the sound of her laughter a lot. He couldn't remember ever laughing after having sex before, but with Rosie, it felt like a natural part of the whole sex experience. And it just made him feel that much better. That much nicer.

Reason number six.

"So I have a proposition for you," she told him.

Really not looking good for getting the hell out, he thought.

"I'm thinking," she said, "that since we both enjoyed ourselves so much this evening, we should get together and do it again soon."

Oh, no, Sam thought. No, no, no, no, no. That was exactly opposite what he'd been thinking himself. Well, okay, he *had* been thinking about how nice it would be to get together and do it again soon—like, for instance, five minutes from now—but he knew that wasn't a *good* idea. As nice as it had been with Rosie…

Well, that was the point. It had been nice with Rosie. And Sam didn't do nice. Plus, he still wasn't sure about her origins. Why did he keep forgetting that part?

"Just what are you asking for, Rosie?" he finally said, telling himself he was *not* sidestepping all the reasons he should be doing his best to completely stamp out this thing with her.

She moved the hand at his belly lower, circling the base of his cock with her fingers. She did nothing more, only held him, but it was enough to mess with Sam's reasoning ability, enough to make him stop thinking about anything other than—

"Sex," Rosie said. "I'm only asking for sex. Nothing more than that. I've missed it, Sam. A lot. And with you, sex is…" She grinned again, but there was something in it this time that hadn't been there before. "It's amazing," she finally told him. "We're good together. Physically, I mean. It just seems natural that we should keep seeing each other. For physical reasons."

It was every man's dream, he thought. A gorgeous, luscious woman with an insatiable, adventurous libido saying she wanted nothing more than to have sex with him whenever the desire struck. So why wasn't Sam jumping on the opportunity? Why was he hesitating? Why was there part of him thinking it might not be such a good idea?

Oh, yeah. Because it would be ethically wrong. Because he didn't know who or what she was or where she came from. Because she made him feel a way he didn't allow himself to feel. It had been a mistake to have sex with Rosie even once. Not just for the wealth of other reasons he'd listed, but because now he knew how incredibly good sex could be, and he'd have to spend the rest of his life knowing what he was missing. To get involved with her any further would be beyond stupid. Beyond unethical. Even if he were only doing it temporarily, and for nothing more than a physical release, to allow this thing with her to go any further would be—

Torture, he thought. It would be torture. And to keep having sex with a woman under false pretenses, to sleep with her while he was investigating her—even if he did have doubts she was guilty of a crime—would be the kind of thing only a lousy son of a bitch would do.

A switch post in the dark recesses of Sam's mental rail yard clicked at that, turning the tracks of his thoughts in a new direction, a direction he told himself not to travel. Journeying down this path of reasoning would have him arriving at a destination he should bypass completely. Because there was a great big sign at that destination that read, "Lousy sons of bitches who don't deserve to be happy welcome." And damned if he didn't already feel right at home.

Rosie's hand at the base of his cock moved higher,

the fingers tightening as they went, making him feel more welcome still. When she reached the head, she palmed it lightly, then hooked her thumb and index finger around the rim, moving up and down in quick, soft, butterfly-like caresses. And just like that, Sam completely forgot what he'd been thinking about, because the images that crashed into his brain were of a much more graphic nature.

"Okay," he heard himself say breathlessly before he could stop the word from coming. "As long as we both go into the agreement knowing what it really is. Sex. Just sex. The physical execution of a physical reaction brought about by a physical attraction. With no expectations beyond that. For however long both of us want to keep the arrangement alive."

The hand pumping the head of his cock paused, and he waited for Rosie to look insulted. Instead, she smiled. "No expectations beyond that," she agreed. "For however long we both want it." Then, taking his cock fully in her hand, she moved down his body and lowered her head, drawing him fully into her mouth.

And that was when the switch post in Sam's mental railyard clicked again, making it impossible for him to turn back.

IN THE WEEK THAT FOLLOWED their agreement, Sam saw quite a bit of Rosie—but only for sex, of course. In addition to having dinner out a couple of nights—at Kathy's Korner Kafé, no less, in full view of everyone—they frequently met for lunch. Often, he went to Rosie's shop with carryout, or she joined him at the station with something she brought herself. And even though they didn't have sex on all those occasions, it went without saying that they were only meeting because of the prospect of sex. Since, in case he hadn't mentioned it, the only reason they continued to see each other was because they both needed a sexual release.

A couple of days, however, one or the other was too busy with too much work or too many obligations, and they didn't see each other at all. And if Sam's mood on those days was a little blacker than it was the rest of the week, it was only because he wasn't getting any sex, and that naturally put a guy in a worse than usual mood. Never mind that he'd had plenty of days like that before Rosie came into his life and they'd never affected his mood at all.

Rosie hadn't come into his life, he quickly reassured himself whenever he found himself thinking that way. They weren't sharing their lives. They were sharing her bed. And her couch. And her floor. And her kitchen countertop. And once, in an especially erotic episode, her washing machine.

Big difference.

In fact, the only reason they even got together for dinner or lunch, he also reassured himself whenever he found himself thinking things he shouldn't be think-ing—such as how instead of feeling like a lousy son of a bitch when he was with Rosie, he felt kind of good— was so they could have sex. Except that they never had sex during their lunch hours, and they always took their time eating dinner before they had sex, because they talked so much, and it took a while to finish.

They never talked about anything important, he reminded himself. They never *shared* things. Just the usual small talk about the origins of the universe and the meaning of life, the philosophical quandary of paper versus plastic and its repercussions on the environment, and why Madonna had to remake *Swept Away* when the original film was flawless and such a socially significant icon of its times. Chitchat stuff like that. Just to have something to do until they could have sex.

That was the *only* reason they tried to see each other every day. To have sex. They'd just both gone so long without, that was all. And there was no one else in Northaven they wanted to have sex with except each other. And the sex they had was so incredibly good. It only made sense that they'd continue to see each other. For sex. They were consenting adults who were eager and adventurous in their sexual pursuits. That they also enjoyed each other's company during the time when they weren't having sex was just bonus.

It wasn't why they kept seeing each other. They did that so they could have sex. In case he hadn't mentioned that already.

As for his rationale that continuing to see Rosie socially—or, rather *sexually*—would be a fitting punishment for a man like him, who deserved nothing more than a temporary, superficial fling with an amazing woman that would leave him wanting her for the rest of his life and remind him of how much he was missing not being able to have her, well…

Actually, that was working out pretty well, too. Because with every day that passed and he didn't hear anything about Rosie from his colleagues out of state or discover anything with his own halfhearted search in Northaven, Sam's growing unease multiplied. The longer he went without new information, the more evident it became that Rosie, whoever she was, wasn't guilty of anything more than keeping secrets she was perfectly entitled to keep. That whatever she had to hide in her past was personal, not criminal. That Sam really was using a perfectly nice woman for sex.

Never mind that it had been her idea. He never should have let it go this far. This thing with Rosie, as incredible as it was, would eventually burn itself out. His knowledge of that was at the heart of every coupling, which only made every coupling that much more intense. Every time with Rosie, he knew, could be his last. Either she would grow tired of him, or he would grow tired of her. Or they would grow tired of each other. Eventually, everything was going to blow up in his face. It just felt too good not to. When it did, it would be a fitting conviction for the crimes of his life. Because he really would spend the rest of his life imprisoned by the haunting reminders of his time with her, and how things could have been.

But Sam wasn't thinking about that as his lunch hour approached two Mondays after his first date with Rosie. He was thinking about a rash of dorm break-ins on campus that looked like the work of someone outside the college community. And sex with Rosie. Not that the rash of break-ins looked like the work of sex with Rosie. That part was just the usual mental drifting off. What Sam was thinking about most was how the break-ins on campus bore some marked similarities to another spate of break-ins that had occurred in a neighboring community this time last year. And sex with Rosie.

Not that those dorm break-ins bore any similarity to sex with Rosie, either. That was mental drifting off again.

He sighed as he looked at a stack of reports that had been sexed—he meant *faxed*—from a detective in the neighboring community for him to look through. Vicky had taken the day off, and his two deputies were both out working cases, so Sam knew he'd be alone most of the afternoon. He could always get a lot of work done when he had the station to himself.

And he could also do a lot of thinking about sex with Rosie.

As if conjured by the thought, she suddenly breezed through the door of the station carrying two bags from Barb's Bohemian Bakery next door that looked full enough to feed two people. He didn't suppose he would ever get used to how beautiful she was. Today, she had that glorious mass of dark copper hair pulled back into a loose ponytail bound at her nape, but it spilled over one shoulder in a rich river of auburn that encircled her breast in a way that made Sam want to mimic the gesture. Her clingy, long-sleeved T-shirt was the color of good red wine, its neck dipping low enough to reveal the upper swells of her breasts. Her flowered skirt flared over her curvy hips, the hem stopping at her knees to reveal the luscious arcs of her calves.

Sam had always considered himself a breast man, but

Rosie had incredible legs, too. Especially when they were draped over his shoulders as he thrust his cock deep inside her or tasted her. His dick twitched in response to the thought, and he suddenly had an appetite for something other than what Rosie had in that bag.

"Feel like taking a break for lunch?" she asked as she made her way across the room to his desk. "I brought sandwiches and sodas."

"Always," he told her, ignoring, as he always did, the little twinge of anguish he felt whenever he saw her and was forced to remember how temporary this thing with her was bound to be. "Who's minding the store?" he asked as she began to unpack the bags. "I'd hate to have to investigate a robbery later."

She waved a hand airily in unconcern. "I locked up and put out a Back At One O'clock sign on the door. It'll be fine."

"But I thought lunch hour was kind of a busy time for you."

"Not on Monday," she told him.

"Nobody comes in to buy flowers to surprise their girlfriends or wives?"

She made a derisive sound. "College guys don't do the flower thing. They bring their girlfriends music download gift cards or lattes. And the married men of Northaven only buy flowers for special occasions or major transgressions. Northaven being the kind of town it is, there aren't that many transgressions. Even Alice and Don are back on an even keel."

"And it was a vibrator, not flowers, that did it," Sam said.

Rosie laughed. "Well, it *is* an awfully good vibrator. Not that I've needed mine lately, mind you," she added with a sly look his way.

"Damn straight," he told her. If he had his way, the only D batteries she had in her future would be for her CD player.

At least for now, he hastily corrected himself. Even in situations where things between two people *weren't* built on a jumble of problems and misconceptions, sex got boring after a while.

Of course, the sex he'd had with other women hadn't been anywhere near as great as the sex he had with Rosie. Sex with her went beyond great. It was spectacular. It was phenomenal. It was extraordinary. It was quite possibly illegal in thirty-eight states. She was just so uninhibited, so insatiable. He'd never known another woman to give so freely of herself, or to take so greedily from him. He liked it. He liked it a lot.

He liked her. He liked her a lot. And it was going to hurt like hell when things finally fell apart. Which, of course, was what he expected. And, of course, what he deserved.

Since Rosie had left her shop unattended, Sam was about to suggest that they take their lunch back there, since any calls that came into the station would be forwarded to his cell phone. But two things happened at almost the same time that prevented him from getting the words out. First, Rosie dropped a napkin on the floor behind his desk and she stooped to retrieve it. And immediately after that, Ed Dinwiddie came through the door.

Not sure why he did it, Sam cupped both hands on Rosie's shoulders to hold her in place, keeping her hidden behind the big desk. He hadn't seen Ed since he'd promised to investigate her, and he was sure that was why the other man was here now. The last thing Sam needed was for Ed to see him having a cozy lunch with her at the station when he was supposed to be proving she was peddling drugs on campus. Certainly he planned to prove to Ed that his suspicions about Rosie were all wrong, but not until Sam could provide concrete evidence, since nothing else was going to dissuade Ed from his convictions.

It occurred to him then that he could just ask Rosie flat out about the discrepancy in her social security number the next chance he got. Hell, they'd reached a point in their relationsh— Uh, he meant in their sexual escapades, of course—that he could ask her something like that. He could make a little joke about it when he did, might even tell her about Ed's suspicions, since Ed was notorious in town for seeing crime where there was none. Sam would tell Rosie he'd only run her social security number to prove to Ed how wrong he was, but there had been some kind of computer glitch—wasn't there always?—that made it look as if she'd never existed anywhere before moving to Northaven, and wasn't that the funniest damned thing she'd ever heard, so really, what was up with the whole social security number thing?

Of course, that didn't solve the problem of what to do about Ed right now. Sam spared a glance down at Rosie, who looked very confused, but he only gave her a silent, meaningful look, hoping she'd understand what he wanted her to do.

"Sam, we need to talk," Ed said as he drew closer to the desk. "You never called me back about—"

"The problem on campus," Sam interrupted the other man before he could say Rosie's name aloud. Even worse than having Ed report him to the state police board for fraternizing with a suspect—which Ed would doubtless do, even though Rosie wasn't suspected of committing a crime—would be having Rosie think Sam suspected her of committing a crime. That would put an even more premature end to their time together than he was already anticipating.

Funny, though, how it wasn't the prospect of never having sex with Rosie again that made his gut clench tight the way it did just then. It was the prospect of never seeing Rosie again. Never talking to her. Never spending time with her. Never having lunch or dinner with her. Never walking through town or the park with her. Never seeing the way she smiled at him or the way her eyes went all soft after he kissed her. Never—

But then, that was the point, right? That he should miss all that. That he *would* miss all that.

"Yeah, Ed, sorry about being out of touch," he hurried on before his thoughts could get maudlin.

He scooted back his chair and hoped Rosie would take the hint and crawl into the small space beneath the big desk where she'd be completely hidden from Ed's view, even if he came around to the side. From the corner of his eye, Sam saw her do just that, so he pulled his chair in again, as close as he could without crowding her.

"I've just been really busy with other cases," he continued. "It's been one of those weeks, you know? But I'm working on it. I just don't have anything new to report."

"But what have you found out about Ro—"

"I ran that name you wanted me to," he interrupted Ed again, "but nothing's come up yet. I've even got a couple of guys in other cities asking around," Sam added when Ed started to open his mouth again. "But I haven't heard a word all week. These things take time, Ed," he added. "People have more than one case to investigate—even me—and other things take priority sometimes. You'll be the first to know as soon as I have something to report."

Ed studied him in silence for a minute, and Sam worried he was going to press the issue. Finally, though, he nodded. "Okay. I guess you're right. And I want to make sure we do this by the book. No shortcuts. Gotta follow procedure."

Like Sam needed for Ed to put that fine a point on it.

He hoped that concluded their conversation and that Ed would go away. Instead, Ed went to Vicky's desk and grabbed her chair, then rolled it back to sit down in front of Sam's.

Oh, great, Sam thought. *Now what?*

"There's something else I wanted to ask you about," Ed said as he pushed the chair closer.

"Can it wait?" Sam asked. "I was about to have lunch."

"Oh, go ahead and eat," Ed said. "I don't want to interrupt."

It was then that Sam noticed Rosie was moving around under his desk. At first, he thought she was just trying to get herself into a more comfortable position.

Then he felt her hand on his shin. And then on his knee. And then on his thigh. And then on his—

Oh, boy.

But she kept on going after palming his cock, up to the buckle of his belt, which she deftly and silently tugged open.

What the hell...?

"It's about Bruno," Ed was saying.

Not that Sam was really listening, since after unfastening his belt, Rosie flicked open the button on his trousers and silently pulled the zipper down. And God help him, even with Ed Dinwiddie sitting on the other side of his desk having no idea what was going on, Sam's cock rose sturdy and strong against his boxers. That, in turn, made it even harder to listen to Ed, who, let's face it, was no picnic to have a conversation with in the first place. What had they been talking about again...?

"...Bruno?" Ed said, turning the word up at the end so that it made a question.

Actually, Sam had never thought about giving his cock a name, and if he had, it certainly wouldn't have been Bruno. It would have been something like Deke or Dirk or Chuck or Rod or—

"Your deputy?" Ed added when Sam still didn't reply. Mostly because Rosie was by then helping his Deke, Dirk, Chuck and Rod out of his boxers and into her hand.

Still, he supposed *deputy* was as good a word for it as any. Though as far as Sam was concerned, *cock* was just fine. And his cock was just fine when he felt Rosie flick her tongue against the head of it. Oh...

Then Sam realized Ed wasn't talking about the thing Rosie was tasting. He wasn't talking about Sam's deputy, Bruno, he was talking about Sam's *deputy, Bruno.*

Oooohhhh, he thought to himself as the realization dawned.

"Oooohhhh," he said aloud as Rosie sucked his cock into her mouth.

Ed narrowed his eyes. "You okay, Sam? You look a little…"

Aroused? Sam wanted to supply for the other man. *Stimulated? Excited? Horny? Like someone's got my dick in her mouth?*

"Off," Ed finally finished.

Wow, that was funny, Sam thought. Because *off* was the last thing he felt when Rosie nibbled the head of his cock with her teeth.

"Listen, Ed," Sam somehow managed to say as Rosie began to run the flat of her tongue up and down the length of his cock. "Can we talk about this some other time? I really need to finish my lunch. As suck…I mean *luck*…would have it, I have a beating…ah, I mean *meeting*…I need to get to." He turned his hand and gave his watch a perfunctory look just as Rosie gave his dick a more than perfunctory suck.

"But Bruno was saying something the other day about maybe resigning, and I was wondering if you were taking applications for his job."

What Sam was taking at the moment he'd just as soon not discuss with Ed. So he only told the other man, "Bruno's been having a rough week." Unlike some people who were currently having the best week of their lives, he added to himself. "Don't listen to him. He's not going to quit. He's a total blowhard."

Which Rosie took as a command, because the minute the word was out of his mouth, she took her oral ministry to new heights.

Ed looked crestfallen at the news, unlike Sam, who was riding a higher crest than he'd felt in a long time.

"Oh," the other man said. "Well, if he does tender his resignation…"

Rosie tendered something then that Sam would never forget. "You'll be the first to know, Head…I mean *Ed,*" Sam assured him.

By some wild miracle, Sam was actually able to exchange a few more sentences with the man until he said his goodbyes and left. As soon as Ed was out the door, Sam pushed his chair out from under the desk, only to have Rosie poke her head out and reach for his cock again.

"What do you think you're doing?" he demanded.

"Eating," she said with a smile as she circled him with sure fingers and drew him toward her mouth again. "Now let me finish," she murmured.

He watched as she gave his cock the same sort of lick she might give a lollipop, curling her tongue around the head before flicking the tip against it. Then she sucked him completely inside and did it again. Sam threaded his fingers into her hair, sifting the silky tresses over his hand, loving the sight of her head moving up and down in his lap as she sucked him into her mouth and released him again. She took him deep enough that he could feel his cock push against the back of her throat when she went down, then the tug of her lips when she came back up again.

The intimacy of the gesture nearly overwhelmed him. Never before had he considered a blow job intimate. Before, they'd always been erotic because they'd felt wrong. Dirty somehow. Forbidden. With Rosie, it felt like the most natural, most loving thing in the world.

When he felt his climax in the pit of his belly surging upward, he said softly, "Rosie, I'm coming."

With one final pull of her mouth, she released him, then wrapped the fingers of both hands around him. She caressed and petted him until he was ready to explode, then she reached for the napkins on the desk and covered him as he came, catching his release in the soft paper.

Sam collapsed against his chair as she cleaned him up and put him back together, thinking about the many ways he would repay her later. That, however, just got him worked up all over again, so he made himself think about something else instead. Glaciers bobbing in the Arctic Ocean. Salmon fighting their way up an icy stream. A Sno-kone down his pants. Ernest Borgnine in a thong. Oh, yeah. That did it. Whoa. Sam wilted completely at that. Rosie kissed him one last time then moved to the other side of the desk, seating herself where Ed had been and unwrapping their sandwiches as if nothing had happened.

"Good God, what was that?" he asked when he trusted himself to speak.

"Well, I hope it was a mind-scrambling blow job," she told him as she placed a sandwich in front of him.

"What? You mean it wasn't? I guess I'll just have to try harder next time."

God help him, his cock started to rise again at the thought of Rosie trying harder. He pushed the thought away and smiled at her. "If Ed had known you were under that desk…"

He stopped right there. If Ed had known she was under that desk, Sam would be answering a call from the State Ethics Board right about now. He had to get his mind back on the matter of Rosie's background and clear things up as soon as possible, and get Ed off both their backs. This week, he promised himself. He'd ask her about her social security number the first chance he had to introduce it into conversation. And he'd touch base with his colleagues in the South one more time. And then…

Well. He guessed he'd just sit back and wait for everything to blow up in his face. And then he'd spend the rest of his life in misery, just as he'd planned.

7

ROSIE WAS BOTTLING UP what was left of her dried ginseng in the back of her shop Tuesday evening when the bell out front rang, announcing the arrival of a customer. She'd been dabbling in other forms of aphrodisiacs besides her teas, wanting to offer her clientele more variety. She'd seen some meager success with incense and baked goods, but what she really wanted was to discover a body oil that would enable the skin to absorb the aphrodisiac subcutaneously. Massage was just such a sensual part of lovemaking and incorporated so many different senses. Touch, sight and smell most notably, but also sound and taste when performed correctly. She'd love to develop a massage oil that would smell and feel wonderful but also infuse the receiver with that added little jolt of arousal that would bring massage to the next level.

So far, however, she hadn't hit on the right combination of herbs and spices. She was hoping that adding a little ginseng extract and upping the amount of mint oil in her most recent recipe would work, and she'd just bottled the final product.

Maybe she could try it out on the customer outside,

she thought as a smile curled her lips. She was sure she'd flipped the Open-Closed sign to the latter position a half hour ago, and the good citizens of Northaven were always good about respecting that, even when she forgot to lock the door.

Save one notable exception.

"Hi," she heard that notable exception call out.

She looked up just as Sam strode through the door that linked the front of her shop with the back, marveling at the bubble of delight that floated up from her belly and popped in her heart, filling it with all kinds of silly, whimsical feelings. The ten days that had passed since their first date—not that she was counting or anything because she never did silly, whimsical stuff like that— had been the best she'd ever known. Not that that was necessarily saying a lot since, before coming to Northaven, there had been few times in Rosie's life that had been particularly good. But toward the end there in Boulder, before everything had blown up in her face with the force of a neutron bomb, she'd been experiencing some very good days indeed. These last ones with Sam, however, made even those pale.

But they were only temporary, she reminded herself, as she invariably had to do whenever she saw him. What the two of them were enjoying was wonderful, but it couldn't last. Good things never did. She'd learned that about life, if nothing else. Twice before, Rosie had thought she had a pretty good thing going. Both times, she'd nearly ended up dead. Until Carl Lorrimer was locked up tight behind bars, she'd never feel safe. And even then, she wasn't sure she'd ever feel completely secure. The Miami crime boss she'd tried to help put behind bars—before he'd bought off everyone he needed to ensure his phony exoneration—had a long memory and a longer reach. Even the federal marshals had been surprised when they had to reinvent and relocate Rosie a second time.

And now here she was, involved with the law again, only in an entirely different way. As a teenager living on the streets of Miami, she'd been leery of cops because she hadn't wanted them to know the truth about her—that she was a runaway who'd committed a handful of petty crimes. But as a young woman who was the star witness in a racketeering and attempted murder case, she'd had to rely on the feds to keep her safe.

She smiled, albeit a little sadly. Maybe things weren't so different with Sam after all. She couldn't share the truth of who she was with him for fear that it might somehow endanger her. Yet being with him made her feel safer than she had for years. Maybe forever.

It wouldn't last, though. She knew that. It was why she'd proposed the arrangement in the first place. Because sex with him had been so good, and she'd missed it so much. Because she knew he felt the same way about her. They could enjoy each other for a little while, until the rosy glow wore off. And then…

Well. She'd just do what she'd been doing all her life. She'd deal.

As always, he looked incredibly sexy, even though he was still dressed in his cop clothes. He came to a halt on the other side of the table where she was working and settled his hands loosely on his hips. He wasn't wearing a gun, because he'd told her he thought it was an unnecessary accoutrement in a town like Northaven, something that had only endeared him to Rosie more. He did, however, keep handcuffs tucked into his belt to the right of the buckle, and, as often happened, her gaze fell upon those.

They were going to have to put those handcuffs to good use sometime, she thought as she always did whenever she saw them. Not that she planned on breaking the law or anything, but she did have some ideas about them that were anything but licit. She just couldn't decide if she wanted to handcuff Sam to the bed first or have him handcuff her. And faceup or facedown? Legs bound, too, or left free?

Oh, there were too many choices to make. They'd just have to try every one of them, that was all.

"Hi," she greeted him back as she absently brushed off the stray flakes of ginseng and kava kava that clung to a T-shirt depicting an advertisement for a fictional French florist. She'd paired it with blue jeans that were also, she noticed, dotted with bits of leaf and twig, which she also quickly scrubbed away.

When she looked up again, Sam's eyes were dark with unmistakable desire, even though she'd been touching herself in a way that was perfectly innocent. Gee, if that turned him on, then tonight was definitely a good night for trying out the massage oil. First things first, however. She had a shop to tidy up.

"Let me help you clean up," he said, as if reading her mind.

She was grateful for the offer, and not just for the

obvious reasons. But also because it meant Sam would have to move to the other side of the table where she was. Rosie always felt better when Sam was physically closer to her. She tried to tell herself it was because his nearness aroused her physically, and physical arousal was a state she'd come to enjoy a lot lately. It *wasn't* because she enjoyed his spiritual and emotional closeness, too. Why, she barely noticed those at all. Really.

Rosie had come to terms a long time ago with the fact that she'd never get close to another human being spiritually *or* emotionally. Hell, she wasn't even sure she was capable of feeling either anyway. Her early life had been void of emotional and spiritual closeness. Her mother had been too busy looking for her next fix, and Rosie didn't know who her father was. She doubted her mother even knew. Attachments, friendships, had been difficult for her back then. Which, she supposed, was one of the reasons she'd been so easily seduced by Carl Lorrimer in the first place. She'd mistaken his lust for love, his sex for comfort, his possessiveness for protection.

When she was young, Rosie had been so naive about human emotions, she hadn't even been able to identify the good from the bad. As an adult, she knew better. For the most part. But she still wasn't sure just how deeply she could feel emotions herself. Though Sam certainly made her feel things she'd never felt before....

"Busy day?" he asked as he helped her clean up her mess. Better still, he helped her forget what she'd been thinking about.

"A little," she said. "With fall planting time here and the holidays around the corner, I have a few more people coming in than usual. And Mrs. Culpepper wants me to do the flowers for her daughter's wedding in June, so that was a nice windfall. I may have to actually hire an employee soon."

"Sounds to me like a reason to celebrate."

Rosie grinned. Over the past ten days, she'd learned that Sam's idea of a celebration generally involved lots and lots of prolonged sex. And his reasons to celebrate had included everything from learning that the soup of the day at Kathy's Korner Kafé was split pea, to seeing socket wrenches on sale at Tom's Totally Tools, to finding a parking space in the empty lot behind her shop.

"I'm up for it if you are," she told him.

Although he didn't say it, she was certain he was up for it, too. In more ways than one. And he probably had been since the minute he entered the store. He was, without question, the most sexual man she'd ever met, and the only one who had been as enthusiastic about sex as she was. Which was saying something, since Rosie had never shied away from sex. With Sam, there was nothing he didn't want to try at least once. And usually a lot more than that. She just felt so incredibly comfortable with him when they were together. Their sex was so natural, so earthy, so easy. It was almost as if they were two halves of one whole, and that, when they came together, that whole unit was excellence personified. They just…fit. Perfectly. She could think of no other way to describe it.

"Your place or mine?" he asked her.

The question was a lot more earth-shattering than it sounded, because so far, they hadn't had sex at Sam's house at all. He always stopped by the shop after work, and either they just never quite made it out again because they were too anxious to be together, or they grabbed a bite to eat in town then headed back to her place because it was closer than his.

Rosie had told herself at first that it was simply a matter of geography and impatience. That her home had always been more convenient to their needs. But as more days went by and Sam never invited her over to his house, she had begun to wonder if there was some reason he simply didn't want her there.

And she'd told herself that was okay, truly. Some people had strange ideas about sex. Some insisted on going to a hotel. Some didn't like to have sex at their partner's home. Some didn't like to bring their partner to their own homes. Sam was one of those last, she'd told herself. It was nothing personal.

Really. It wasn't. Honest.

Hey, it wasn't like they had a relationship. They'd started this thing because they'd wanted to enjoy great sex together. That was what they were doing. That was all it would ever be. Rosie had no desire to tie her life to Sam's in some domestic ideal that didn't even exist as far as she was concerned. It was okay if she never went to his house. His house wasn't what she wanted from him. Sex was what she wanted from him. Only sex. Nothing more.

Really. She did. Honest.

So why did she experience such giddy delight now at the prospect of visiting his home? she asked herself. Because she was going to have great sex there, she immediately answered her own question. Possibly even involving handcuffs. What wasn't there to feel giddy about?

"Your place," she said decisively. Then she waited to see if he'd been bluffing and would try to change her mind.

"Sounds good," he immediately replied. "I got a couple of steaks on my lunch hour and went home to start them marinating. And I have a good piñot noir I've been saving for a special occasion. It's supposed to be a nice night. Unseasonably warm. We can grill out."

Rosie hoped her surprise didn't show on her face. What he'd just described sounded like the quintessential cozy evening at home, something that would have terrified many men. She told herself it should terrify her, too. Instead, she found herself kind of liking the prospect. Strangest of all, it wasn't the sex that would doubtless come after dinner that created the warmth inside her. It was the opportunity to simply spend time with Sam.

"Help me put all this stuff away, and I'll be ready," she said.

He helped her carry everything to the cabinet where she kept her supplies, and it was only when Rosie opened it that she remembered her basket of special orders also sitting inside. Mostly because that was where her gaze fell, onto the assortment of plastic Ziploc bags that were filled with dried herbs awaiting the little cloth sacks she put them in before turning them over to her customers. Wow, she thought. She'd never really paid attention, but to the casual observer, they looked like bags of marijuana. That could really get her into trouble if the wrong eyes happened to fall upon th—

Immediately, she slammed the cabinet door shut,

nearly catching Sam's hand in the process because he was about to put a bottle of kava kava inside.

"Yow," he said as he withdrew his hand just in time. "What's wrong?"

"Spider," she said. "Really, really big spider in there. Run to the front of the shop. I've got some bug spray on a shelf behind the counter."

He grinned. "No need for bug spray, little lady," he said in a passably good John Wayne voice, hitching up his trousers and puffing up his chest. "I'll take care of that nasty spider for ya. Just get me a rolled-up newspaper or something."

"Rolled-up newspaper won't be enough, pardner," she told him. "It's a really, really, really big spider. Like supersized spider. The kind of spider you only see in postatomic apocalypse movies. That spider could take your head clean off. You might want to go back to the station for your gun."

Sam chuckled at that. "C'mon, Rosie. Stand aside. I've faced down a lot worse than big bugs in my life."

But instead of following his instructions, she moved in front of the cabinet. "It could be poisonous," she said. "It had that look to it."

He didn't move, only cocked a dark eyebrow at her.

"Really," she said. "And I couldn't stand the thought of you being poisoned by a spider. Or your hand being taken clean off. I have plans for you—and your hand—later."

That, finally seemed to do the trick, because he rolled his eyes, sighed heavily, and went to retrieve the bug spray. Which, Rosie knew, ought to keep him for a while, since there was no bug spray in the front of the shop on account of she didn't believe in using chemicals on any living things.

Then she had to wonder at her behavior, panicking the way she had. It wasn't as though she actually *had* marijuana stowed in her cabinet. Even if Sam mistook her aphrodisiacs for cannabis—which, incidentally, was used as an aphrodisiac in some cultures—a simple lab test would prove it was nothing more than dried herbs. So what was the big deal?

Belatedly, she realized she could have just told him it was potpourri, since she'd already told him that was what she made for the college girls. No quick-on-her-feet thinker, she. Nevertheless, she took advantage of Sam's absence to withdraw the big basket and stow it in the neighboring cabinet, out of sight.

She supposed it was just a knee-jerk reaction. She'd had enough run-ins with the law—even before Sam starting running her in in an entirely different and much more enjoyable way—that she had an unnaturally strong reaction to anything that might be misconstrued as criminal behavior on her part. Truth be told, it was surprising she'd ever been attracted to Sam in the first place, thanks to her teenage wariness of cops in general. She told herself it must have been because of the dearth of available men in Northaven otherwise. Of course, it didn't hurt that he was powerfully sexy. Or that she'd gone more than a year without having sex before even making his acquaintance. By the time Sam came into her life, she wouldn't have been surprised if she'd been wanting to have sex with kitchen appliances.

Oh, wait. She *had* been having sex with kitchen appliances. Well, there you go then. That explained it.

"I don't see any bug spray out here," Sam called from the front of the shop. Then a moment later, from closer behind Rosie came, "I did find a magazine to roll up, though."

She spun around to find him right behind her, holding the latest issue of *Horticulture Today.*

"Not that!" she cried as he began to roll it up. "It has a riveting article about organic African violet production that I want to save."

Sam didn't know whether she was serious or not, which just went to show how much he knew. Growing African violets organically was a real bitch.

"Besides," she added, "I was mistaken." She opened the cabinet again, pulling the door wide. "It wasn't a spider after all. It was just a big glob of fertilizer. I am so embarrassed. Sorry about that."

The way Sam looked at her then, he seemed to be thinking that wasn't the only big glob of fertilizer he'd been subjected to in the last few minutes. But Rosie only smiled brightly and turned to retrieve the bottles of herbs from the table where they'd set them. One by one, she put them away, humming lightly under her breath as she did in an attempt to divert Sam's attention from her bizarre behavior.

Unfortunately, she realized much to her dismay that what she was humming was Fleetwood Mac's "Tell Me Lies," so she quickly shut herself up.

When she turned around again, she saw the bottle of massage oil she'd just whipped up still sitting on the table, so she gathered it up and collected her purse from her desk. "I'm ready when you are," she said.

He dipped his head toward the bottle in her hand. "What's that?"

"A little something we can enjoy later," she told him.

"So then it's not salad dressing?" he asked. "Nothing edible?"

"Oh, it's edible," she assured him as she threaded her arm through his and began to lead him toward the front door. "But there won't be any dressing involved when we use it."

ROSIE COULD HAVE SAID the same thing about Sam's house that he had said about her apartment. It didn't reflect him or his character at all. It was nice enough, but Spartan, with little color and less decoration. Although it was masculine, it was masculine in a generic way that would have been appropriate for nearly every man. Were she the one living here, she would have immediately added more color and texture and—

But she wasn't living here, she quickly reminded herself. This was Sam's place, and he'd obviously furnished it in a way that suited him, even if the way he'd furnished it didn't suit him at all. Still, it was curious, the absence of so much. Rosie knew why *she* didn't have more of the accessories he'd noted weren't present in her house. There were no photos because there was no family, and her friends in Miami had been street kids who were even more troubled than she'd been herself. Not to mention she didn't want any reminders of that time in her home anyway. Although she did have some fond memories of her experiences in Colorado—she'd even managed to make a few friends there—she'd been forced to leave so quickly after the attempt on her life that she hadn't had time to pack up anything other than the essentials.

At this point, she supposed she'd just been uprooted often enough over the years that now she was hesitant to get too attached to anything or anyone. Well, most anyones. But she couldn't help wondering why Sam hadn't surrounded himself with the markers and milestones of his own life.

He'd had a job he enjoyed in Boston and must have had plenty of friends in his precinct. Cops were a tight-knit bunch, she knew, having witnessed more than her fair share of them in the past. He was close enough to his mother that he sent her flowers, and he spoke of her with clear affection. He'd told Rosie his father passed away eight years ago, but that he'd had a good relationship with him while he was alive. Yet there were no photos of Sam's friends or family in his house, either. No citations of a job well done. No sports memorabilia or indications of a favorite hobby. And the house was a lot tidier than she would have expected, too, as if he were afraid even being messy might reveal too much about him.

Now, as she leaned back against the deck railing and watched him light the grill, she twirled her wineglass by its stem and told herself to just enjoy the evening. He'd changed out of his uniform and into a pair of blue jeans and a well-worn sweatshirt with "UMass" stretched across the chest. He'd also brought out a denim jacket for Rosie to put on, since the air had turned cooler after their arrival. She tried not to feel too snug as she wrapped it more securely around herself and inhaled the scent of Sam that clung to it.

His house abutted the park, so his backyard opened into a thick row of trees that were filled with evening birds chirping to greet the oncoming night. The sun had dipped below the tree line, bathing the house in shadow, so he'd lit a citronella candle at each corner of the deck, even though bug season was well behind them. The lemony scent of the candles was nice, as was the soft jazz drifting through the open kitchen window behind them. The cool October breeze caressed her face and sifted through her hair, bringing with it the tiniest hint of the winter ahead.

It really was a lovely evening. And although she did her best to stop the thought from forming—really, she did—all Rosie could think was, *I could get used to this. I could definitely get used to this.*

She pushed the impression out of her mind as soon as it gelled. She would not be getting used to this. She never got used to anything. Because things could be ripped away from you much too quickly. And invariably, they were.

"Just give the charcoal a little while," Sam said, stirring her from her thoughts, "and then I'll put the steaks on." He smiled after sipping his own wine and added, "It shouldn't take long, since I'm sure you're not one of those barbarians who likes her steak well-done."

"Medium rare should do," she told him.

He winced even at that, but said nothing.

She smiled. "Obviously, you're one of those barbarians who likes his steak still bleeding from a gaping wound."

"Actually, I like my steak to go a few rounds of poker with me before I throw it on the grill, but tonight I'll make an exception since the company is so enjoyable."

"I'll play poker with you," she offered.

He grinned. "The kind of poker I'd play with you would make us end up skipping dinner, and I'm really in the mood for a good, tender piece of meat."

She feigned affront. "You'd just better be talking about the steak, mister."

"Yeah, that, too," he said, laughing.

Silence descended again after that, but it wasn't awkward, the way it might have been. That could only mean the two of them were comfortable enough together now that they didn't feel the need to fill every quiet moment with talk. They could just enjoy the quiet moments for what they were. A chance to be together.

Even if it was only going to be temporary, she hastily reminded herself.

"I like your house," she finally said, echoing his sentiment that first night in her apartment.

"Thanks," he said.

Even though she'd told herself she wouldn't do it, she added, "But you know, I could say the same thing about your place that you said about mine."

He looked confused. "What's that?"

"It doesn't say anything about who you are."

He said nothing for a moment, only sipped his wine in a way that made her think he was stalling. Finally, he told her, "I'm not much of a decorator, that's all."

"But since you grew up in Boston, I'd think you'd

have lots of stuff you would have wanted to bring with you to Northaven."

He shrugged, but there was nothing casual about the gesture. "I haven't finished unpacking yet."

"Or maybe you're like me," she said. "And you just don't like to have a lot of reminders hanging around."

She didn't add that it might also be because, like her, he was afraid things might go wrong so quickly and so badly that he wouldn't have time to pack.

Even though he moved across the deck to stand beside her, he said nothing in response to her comment.

She told herself to let it go, but instead, she asked, "Why did you feel like you had to leave the Boston police force after—" She hesitated a beat before finishing, "After what happened to Roni. I mean, I don't want to make it out to be routine, or diminish it in any way. But surely that wasn't the first time you witnessed some terrible tragedy like that in your job."

He blew out a long, weary breath, as if he were finally resigned to having to talk about what had happened. Rosie didn't want to push him to tell her anything he didn't want to talk about. But she hoped he would be comfortable enough with her to share—or rather, talk about—the experience. Mostly because she wanted to share—or rather, talk about—some of her experiences with him, too. She was just still too timid to be the one who went first.

"No, it wasn't the first time," Sam told her. "Unfortunately, during my ten years as a vice cop, I ran into dozens of kids like Roni. There seemed to be more every year. And I don't want to say most of them were lost causes, because no one is ever completely irredeemable, but a lot of them were just so damaged it almost seemed like they could never be fixed, you know?"

Rosie nodded. She did know. Probably even better than Sam did. She'd known a few kids like that herself when she was living on the streets.

"But there was something about Roni that was different," he continued. "She was...stronger. I don't know any other way to put it. Where that kind of life killed off the spirit in most kids right away, there was still a spark in her that was so obvious. She could still laugh about stuff. Still think about her future." He met Rosie's gaze levelly in the darkness. "She was such a smart-ass, you know? Funny as hell. And it's been my experience that smart-asses usually outlast everyone else. In Roni's case, it was probably what got her killed. I thought if anyone could get out of that life and rebuild a better one, it was Roni. That her life got snuffed out instead..."

He sighed heavily again and dropped his gaze to the wine in his glass. "I just couldn't do the job anymore after that," he finished softly. "Every time I went out on the streets, I found myself looking for her. And every time I saw another kid standing in an alley or on a street corner, I felt myself pulling back emotionally. Not wanting to get involved with them because they were probably bound for the same fate."

He looked up and gazed at Rosie again through the twilit darkness, the flicker of the candle beside them reflecting in his hair and his eyes and deep in the blood-red wine of his glass. He looked haunted and hunted, desperate and depressed. And more than anything, she wanted to pull him close and hold him, and tell him everything would be all right.

But that would be a lie, she knew. Things were never all right. Sam knew that as well as she did.

His voice grew quiet as he continued. "Once a cop starts pulling away from the job, Rosie, that's the end of it. When I realized I couldn't give it everything I had anymore, I had to quit. And I knew I had to go someplace where I wouldn't have to worry about getting involved with people who might meet a violent end. Someplace innocent. Someplace clean. Someplace where the people didn't do things to each other like they do on the mean streets of the city."

Something turned over inside Rosie at his words, and she smiled. They'd both come to Northaven for similar reasons, she thought, and they'd found the same things. Comfort. Safety. Security.

Sanctuary.

They'd both become jaded and weary by the circumstances of their lives. They'd both seen too much of the world's underbelly, and not enough of its light. They'd both needed a second chance. They'd both needed to be remade. And Northaven, with its crooked, cobbled sidewalks, and its gazebo in the park, and its striped soda shoppe awnings, and its innocent inhabitants had been their perfect Thornton Wilder renovation. Their *Saturday Evening Post* salvation. Their opportunity to start over to be the very best people they could be.

They were both better people for having come here, she thought. And maybe that was all that was important.

"When I saw that the position of police chief was

open here," Sam went on, "I knew it was exactly what I wanted. The town may have needed a new chief, but I needed the town more."

Rosie understood completely. She'd needed Northaven, too, for the same reasons he did. There was an innocence and sweetness about the place that made it seem impossible for menace and malice to thrive. She'd witnessed enough of both—she'd experienced enough of both—that she never wanted to suffer through any of it again. The town had healed her in a way. The same way it was healing Sam.

No wonder the two of them had been drawn to each other, she thought further. On some level, they must have recognized they were two of a kind. She just wished she knew what they were supposed to do about that now.

IN SPITE OF THE CHILL that descended with the setting sun, Sam and Rosie enjoyed dinner and the rest of the piñot on the deck in companionable conversation. Sam left the lid up on the grill to offer some meager heat, but he suspected it was something else that really kept them warm. Strangely, he didn't think it was the sexual undercurrent that always seemed to flow between them. Because for the last several days, there had been something else flowing between them, too. Something that was, surprisingly, even stronger than the sexual undercurrent. He just wasn't sure he could put a name on what exactly it was. Or maybe it was that he didn't want to put a name on it.

Whatever, he thought impatiently. In any event, it was what had made him invite Rosie to his place for dinner tonight. She'd looked surprised when he'd extended the offer to come here, but she couldn't have been any more surprised to hear the invitation than he'd been to realize earlier in the day how much he wanted to extend it. Now, as they stowed the last of the dishes in the dishwasher and he flipped it on, it occurred to him that, with Rosie here, his house felt a lot more comfortable than it ever had before.

Sex, he reminded himself. That was all the two of them were supposed to be having together. Funny, though, how, tonight especially, it felt like so much more.

He thought about opening a second bottle of wine for them to take back out onto the deck, then discovered there was something else he thirsted for more. So without a word, he pulled Rosie into his arms. She looked surprised for a second... But only a second. Then she melted into him, tilting her head back to greet him as he lowered his mouth to hers.

This kiss wasn't as passionate as the ones that generally led to their lovemaking, but Sam felt the familiar heat in his belly just the same. It was slower to rise this time, however, and instead of firing through his body like a rocket shot, it seeped leisurely, comfortably into his chest and his groin, then parts beyond. She just felt so good to hold. So Sam enjoyed the holding a little longer, slanting his mouth one way then the other over hers, skimming his hands over her back and shoulders and waist. Rosie opened one hand over his chest and curled the other around his nape, tilting her head back even more to grant him freer access.

He didn't know how long they stood there in his

kitchen just kissing, but, inevitably the kissing turned to more intimate touching. The palm Sam had been skimming over Rosie's back brushed lower, over the delicate curve of her ass and up again. Her hand on his chest moved lower, too, flattening itself over the ridge in his jeans that had risen while he kissed her. When she pushed her fingers harder against him, his cock swelled higher, as if it were rising to greet her. In response, Rosie began to tug at his belt to free it, an action Sam performed for her, as well.

Together, they opened each other's blue jeans, and together, they dipped their hands inside to stroke each other's flesh. Sex almost always began this way with them. They petted and fondled, touched and caressed, until both were damp with the prelude of their later release. Rosie found the head of Sam's cock and palmed it, then moved her hand lower to circle the long shaft with sure fingers. He in turn slipped a finger inside her wet slit, gliding it in and out every time she moved her hand on him.

Rosie groaned her satisfaction, then, pushing herself up on tiptoe, whispered, "I know we just had dinner, but I'd love it if you ate me for dessert."

She didn't need to ask him twice.

Together they shed her jeans and panties, then Sam helped her onto the counter and pulled up a chair from the kitchen table to seat himself between her legs. Placing a hand on the inside of each thigh, he pushed her legs apart and leaned forward. The dark musky scent of her surrounded him, intoxicated him, made him hunger for her even more. Without hesitation, he covered her sex with his mouth, lapping at the hot flesh with the flat of his tongue, licking the deep folds with long, leisurely tastes. When he found the sensitive nub of her clit, he flicked it with the tip of his tongue, smiling at her gasp of surprise. As he returned to lavish, thorough tasting, she hooked her legs over his shoulders and tangled her fingers in his hair, silently indicating she didn't want him to stop. Which was fine with Sam. He could eat Rosie all night if that was what she wanted.

He felt her legs begin to tremble then, and knew she was about to come. So he gave his complete attention to her little clit, flicking it with dozens of soft, butterfly caresses until her fingers tightened in his hair and she cried out her completion. Then he moved his mouth to her thighs, brushing his lips lightly along the soft skin, reveling in the provocative scent of her release.

"Again, Sam," she whispered weakly from above him. "Make me come again. I want to come a dozen times tonight. And I want to start all over again in the morning."

He helped her off the counter and kissed her, thrusting his tongue into her mouth so that she could enjoy the taste of herself as much as he had. She sucked his tongue in deeper, and her breathing compounded, and she rubbed her entire body against his. As she kissed him, she tucked her hand into his jeans again and curled her fingers around his cock, stroking the length of him before rubbing her thumb lightly over the head.

A bolt of heat shot through him at her touch. But it was nothing compared to the shudder of fire that rocked him when she tore her mouth from his and told him, "Take me now, Sam. Right now. Right here."

He chuckled as he kissed her again, then asked, "What is it about the kitchen that makes us so aroused?"

"It's not just the kitchen," she reminded him. "I want to have you in the living room, too. And the dining room. And the office. And the garage. But for now, the kitchen will do." She pushed herself up on tiptoe and whispered, "Take me from behind this time."

Sam's cock jumped higher at her words, then surged to full erection when she turned around and gripped the countertop, bending at the waist to thrust her ass toward him. He covered it with both hands and stroked her, and she sighed at the contact, a long, lusty, wanton sound that came from the back of her throat.

She watched him over her shoulder as he settled a hand between her shoulder blades and urged her to bend over even more. He bent her until her top half lay flat on the countertop, and she curled her fingers more fiercely along its edge. He traced the elegant line of her spine with one finger, halting at the crease of her ass before retracing the line upward again. He freed his cock from his jeans and, cradling her hips in his hands, pushed his body forward, burying himself in her wet heat. Her cry of delight joined his at the depth of his penetration, and he stilled himself for a moment so that they could adjust their bodies to the position. But Rosie pushed herself backward again, something that drove him deeper still, and, unable to help himself, Sam began to move. Fast. Deep. Hard.

Again and again, he thrust into her from behind, his hands splayed open over her back, holding her in place as he jerked his hips forward. She gasped with each new penetration, and he panted with every thrust, until he felt his own orgasm begin to build. A hot coil inside him began to twist tighter with each new penetration, then rocketed to a near-blinding explosion of joy. His release was hot, hurried, profound. He spilled himself inside her until he had nothing left to give. Then he fell forward, covering her back with his front, his shirt as damp with perspiration as hers was.

The soft breeze blowing through the window quickly cooled them, reminding Sam where they were. Lifting himself from Rosie, he withdrew from her, feeling as though he'd lost something very important. She straightened along with him, and he pulled her into his arms, wrapping them over her back until he couldn't draw her any closer.

He couldn't remember ever holding a woman that way before. Yeah, he'd put his arms around women, and he'd even hugged them from time to time. But he'd never wanted to have one nestled close to him, completely enfolded in his embrace. Much to his surprise, he discovered he liked the position. A lot. In fact, it may just become his new favorite.

"Bed," Rosie said, the word muffled against Sam's chest. "Maybe we should try the bed next."

He smiled. "We are. We have a long night ahead of us."

He felt more than saw her responding smile. "Oh, I do like the sound of that."

Within minutes, they were naked and in his bed, Sam lying flat on his stomach, Rosie straddling him as she held the open bottle of what she'd told him was massage oil over his back.

She laughed softly as she said, "I told you there wouldn't be any dressing when we used this."

"Believe me," he replied, "I'll take this over a salad any day of the week."

Rosie tipped the bottle to dribble oil over Sam's back, and he hissed at what must have been the too-cool temperature, even though she'd tried to warm the small bottle between her hands before opening it. Filling her palm with a final small pool, she set the bottle on the nightstand, then rubbed her palms together briskly to at least warm that. He groaned his satisfaction as she pushed her fingers into his soft flesh, the combination of his skin and her rubbing making the oil heat nicely as she spread it from shoulder to shoulder and neck to waist.

The soft fragrance of mint and cinnamon surrounded her as she massaged him, leaning her body forward to rub her hands down his arms, something that caused her naked breasts to push into his back. Her skin tingled where the spicy oil clung to her, puckering her nipples until they stood erect. As she pulled her hands back down the length of Sam's back, Rosie drew her hands into the juncture of her own legs and skimmed her fingers against her own heated flesh. The oil made her tingle there, as well, and she grew damp in response.

Back and forth, up and down, she pushed her hands into Sam's muscular flesh, mixing the massage oil with her own release as she touched first him, and then herself. Before long, she felt the tug of a climax welling in her belly, and she levered herself off of Sam to turn him onto his back. She needed him inside her. Soon.

But he looked back at her with languid passion,

seeming in no hurry to couple with her. She was about to feel cheated, but he grinned a very wicked grin and murmured thickly, "I love the way you touch me, but now it's your turn."

Well, that sounded promising, she thought. Nevertheless, she asked, "My turn?"

He nodded slowly. "I want to watch you touch yourself. I'd love to see how you get yourself off when you're alone."

"But you told me I wouldn't be needing my Xtacy 2000 as long as you're around," she told him.

"And you don't need it now," he replied. "I don't want to see what a vibrator can do to you. You said it was dynamite in the right hands, so let's see what those hands can do without it."

Rosie had never done that for a man before, but now she discovered she found the idea rather…arousing. She thought about it for a moment, then smiled. "All right."

She moved to the head of the bed with her back against his headboard, spread her legs wide and dropped her hand between them. The soft hair at the apex of her thighs was damp with her arousal, so her fingers slid easily into the folds of her flesh. She sighed as she drew a few slow circles with her middle finger, then murmured with pleasure as she inserted a finger inside herself. Sam's eyes grew darker as he watched her, and his cock leaped higher between his legs. And something about that just made Rosie feel more excited still.

As she caressed her sex with one slow hand, she moved the other to her breast, capturing her nipple with her thumb and forefinger to give it a gentle pinch.

Plucking it softly, she pushed her palm a little faster between her legs and rubbed herself harder, sliding her entire hand back and forth over her swollen flesh. Oh... It felt so good....

As erotic as it was to Sam to watch Rosie finger and palm herself, it was the look on her face that was nearly his undoing. Her eyes were closed, her lips were parted, and her cheeks were flushed dark red. She moaned again, a thick, wanton sound, then grabbed her entire breast with one hand and squeezed hard. When he dropped his gaze again, he saw that she was driving her middle and index fingers in and out of herself fast and deep. Finally, she moved the hand at her breast between her legs, too, and using both, one inside herself and one stroking her sweet clit, she brought herself to orgasm a second time.

He waited until her shudders subsided, waited until she was smiling a dreamy little smile. Then, "You ready to come again?" he asked her.

She nodded, extending her hand toward him in a silent indication that he should tell her what to do. Helping her to her knees, he positioned them so that she knelt before him. Placing his open hand between her shoulder blades, he urged her forward until she was on all fours, then he pushed gently again until her shoulders were on the mattress and her ass was in the air.

She had an incredible ass, he thought as he skimmed his hands open over each of her buttocks, pushing them apart and closing them again, massaging, caressing, squeezing. He stole a moment to lean forward and run his mouth over the elegant curves, dragging soft kisses over one side, flicking his tongue over the creamy skin of the other. Then he straightened and moved closer behind her.

"Spread your legs apart," he instructed her. "Wider," he added after she did.

She did as he told her to, spreading her legs as wide as she could, watching him over her shoulder as he entered her from behind. He skimmed his hands over her ass as he buried himself in her slick chasm, his thumb creasing the two globes to trace a line up and down and back again. As he penetrated her more deeply, his thumb found her other opening and plunged inside, and he heard her gasp at the depth of the dual penetrations. She pushed her ass back, then forward again, mimicking his rhythm with her own. As he felt the shudders of another climax shaking him, Sam drove his cock into her wet canal as deeply as he could, and thrust in his thumb deeper still.

Even as he spilled himself hotly inside her, he wanted her again.

He would never have enough of her, he realized then. For as long as he lived, he would always want Rosie. Always need Rosie. Always dream about Rosie.

This thing with her had to stop, he told himself as he collapsed beside her. It had to. Because it wasn't just sex anymore. It was something else. Something that was making him happy. Something that was making him feel good. Something that made him look forward to the sort of future he didn't deserve and certainly hadn't earned. Being happy and feeling good wasn't part of his plan at all.

It was one thing for Sam to use temporary sex with Rosie as a way to castigate himself for his failure to protect people like Roni. To tempt himself with—and then deny himself—the sort of happiness people like Roni would never know themselves.

It was another thing entirely for Sam to fall in love.

Soon, he promised himself. Very, very soon. He just had to look for the right moment, that was all. The way he was still trying to find the right moment to ask her about her social security number...

8

TWO WEEKS TO THE DAY after asking Sam to go out with her, Rosie lay on her side in her bed and watched him sleeping soundly beside her. The lamp over which she'd tossed a fringed shawl to mute the light bathed both their bodies in an amber glow, and rain pattered softly against the window above her bed. When she inhaled, she smelled the lavender potpourri on her nightstand that was supposed to relax her, and, even better, the distinctive fragrance of Sam. His chest rose and fell with his easy respiration, and his warm breath danced against her neck every time he exhaled. She felt safe and protected and secure with him beside her. As if nothing in her life would ever go wrong again.

Panic rose at the back of her throat at the realization.

He should have looked silly lying there, his square jaw shadowed by a day's growth of beard nestled into the pillowcase decorated with tiny rosebuds. But the feminine backdrop only enhanced his rugged features. A single lock of dark hair had tumbled down on his forehead, and she couldn't resist reaching over to gently brush it back. When she did, he sighed sleepily and circled her wrist with loose fingers to move her hand away. But he didn't let go. Still sleeping, he pulled her hand to his mouth and kissed her palm, then tucked it under his against the pillow.

Her panic multiplied.

Rosie should have felt as peaceful as her surroundings. But it was that very serenity that generated her fear. Less than half an hour ago, she and Sam had indulged in a fierce sexual coupling, and now they were lying side by side in her bed, as calmly as if they slept together every night. That was what scared her. That it felt so comfortable, so natural to be here with him like this. Because she wanted to go to bed this way every night. And wake up this way every morning. For the rest of her life.

She had been telling herself that what she had with Sam was completely sexual in nature. The physical execution of a physical reaction brought about by a physical attraction. Yes, she'd liked him from the start. Yes, she'd enjoyed his company. Yes, she'd hoped they could remain friends once their affair was over. It had still all been based on sex. She was making up for lost time and storing up for the bleak, copulation-free winter that was sure to come once she and Sam grew tired of each other. It was just sex. Just sex.

Just sex.

She expelled a single, joyless chuckle. As if sex with Sam could ever be *just* anything.

She realized that now, too late. He wasn't the sort of man a woman could just have sex with. He was too complicated, too interesting, too decent, too kind, too sweet. Too human. He was the kind of man women fell in love with. And Rosie was no exception.

She, who had never loved anyone in her life, was in love with Sam Maguire. And she had no idea what to do about it.

Her instincts screamed at her to do what she'd always done when she found herself in a position of being scared, panicked and confused. Run. Run fast. Run far. Run until there were thousands of miles between her and whatever it was that threatened her. From Florida to Colorado. From Colorado to Massachusetts. Run away and start all over and build another new life from scratch.

But Rosie was tired of running. And she liked where she was now. Even more important, she liked *who* she was now. She'd rebuilt and revamped and rewired herself so many times, she'd suffer character overload if she tried to do it again. She didn't want to do it again. She'd taken different parts of her different identities over the years—from the wild teenager to the frightened college student to the savvy businesswoman to the nurturing florist—and melded them into the woman she was now. The woman she wanted to remain. But now that woman had fallen in love. And there wasn't a single part of Rosie that knew how to deal with it.

Especially when she realized the man beside her might not feel the same way at all.

As SAM MADE his morning walk to the police station two weeks to the day after agreeing to go out with Rosie—this time leaving from Rosie's home instead of his own, something he seemed to be doing rather a lot of lately—he realized he felt a little…off. For one thing, his vision was messed up, because everything around him looked a little crisper, a little more colorful, a little more vivid than usual. And there was something wrong with his legs, because his pace was slower than it was most days. There was a tightness in his chest he'd never felt before. Nothing painful, but it was definitely something different. His mind kept wandering, too. Where he'd normally spend his walk to work ticking off mentally everything he needed to do today, instead, he kept thinking about Rosie. About how she smelled like a fresh bouquet of flowers, even when she wasn't working in her shop. And how soft she was, no matter where he touched her. And how she uttered that incredibly erotic little sound every time he slipped a finger inside her.

He lifted a hand to his forehead, because now he felt feverish, too, warm all over, as if he was running a major temperature. What was really weird, though, was that in spite of everything that seemed to be wrong with him, Sam felt really, really good. And that, perhaps, was the most telling thing of all. Clearly, he was profoundly off his game today. He wondered if there was something going around. Maybe he should make an appointment with the doctor. Tell him, "Hey, Doc, I have a problem. I feel really good. That's gotta be bad, right?"

It took the rest of his walk to the station, but Sam finally diagnosed his condition. He wasn't sick. He was happy. Genuinely, utterly, irrevocably happy. It had been so long since he'd experienced the feeling—hell, he didn't know that he ever *had* really experienced the feeling—that he honestly didn't recognize it at first. But all the symptoms were there: warm heart, outbreak of optimism, paralysis of pessimism, rash of exuberance, blindness to negativity. And at the root of it, the absolute conviction that nothing in his life would ever go wrong again.

Man. He was terminal. He was going to need unlimited refills of Rosie if he wanted to survive.

The recognition of that stopped him dead in his tracks, his hand flattened on the door to the station, awaiting his push to open it. Unlimited refills of Rosie? he echoed to himself. As in…a lifetime of Rosie? As in…ever after with Rosie? As in…*happily* ever after with Rosie?

What the…?

Understanding dawned on him then, like a two-by-four to the back of his head. He was in love with Rosie, he thought. His genuine, utter, irrevocable happiness was the result of his genuine, utter, irrevocable love for her. Because it wasn't just his libido that had been feeling satisfied lately. It was the rest of him, too. In fact, parts of him he hadn't even known *could* be satisfied had been feeling pretty damned good since he'd started seeing more of Rosie. And they were parts that had nothing to do with sex.

The only thing that could make a person feel this good, inside and out, upside and down, in body and in spirit, had to include more than just the sex organs. It had to include other organs, too. Organs like the brain. And, more to the point, the heart. To feel this soul-deep sense of well-being, more than one's libido had to be engaged. Somewhere over the past two weeks, Sam had surrendered more of himself to Rosie than he'd realized, more than he ever intended to share. What was supposed to have been just sex between them had turned into something more. Way more. Infinitely more. And he, for one, had no idea what to do about it.

Love, he thought again as he pushed open the door to the station and forced his feet to move forward. Was that really possible? For a man pushing forty to fall in love for the first time? Find happiness for the first time? Could it really be that somewhere, somehow, for some reason, someone was rewarding him in a way he'd never thought he'd be rewarded? Because what greater gift could there be than to feel this way? Man, he really did want to feel like this for the rest of his life.

And then another thought hit him. This time like a steel I beam to the back of his head. If Rosie was a reward, and if he had fallen in love with her—and indeed, she felt like way more than a reward and he felt way more than in love with her—then it meant Sam was allowing himself to feel entitled to a reward. Entitled to fall in love. And if that were true, then it could only mean—

He'd forgiven himself, he thought with astonishment. For what he let happen to Roni in Boston.

Hand still flat on the door, he took a moment to think about that. He'd felt responsible for what had happened to Roni. Truth be told, he still didn't think he'd done enough for her. But he also realized that her death wasn't entirely his fault. He wasn't the one who'd lifted a hand to her. And he'd done everything he reasonably could to help her. Maybe, just maybe, it was time to let himself start dealing with that. Because there was at least one person in the world who seemed to think he was worth the effort. Otherwise, she wouldn't be spending her nights making such sweet love with him.

"Hey, Chief."

So preoccupied was he by the epiphanies exploding like fireworks in his brain that Sam didn't hear Vicky's greeting until she was standing right behind him.

"Forget your key again?" she asked as she jingled the ones she held in her hand. "Don't worry. I've got mine."

As she reached past him to unlock the door he hadn't even thought about unlocking himself, all Sam could think was, *I've got mine, too. Now I just need to know if Rosie wants to keep me as much as I want to keep her.*

Epiphanies notwithstanding, once he managed to focus his attentions where they needed to be focused— at least, for now—Sam's morning progressed as mornings usually did in the Northaven Police Station— slowly and uneventfully. Until the phone on Vicky's desk rang, and she told him the call was for him, a detective in Miami by the name of Stu Dorfman. That was when Sam's pulse quickened and his heart began to race. And that was when a feeling of something chilly and heavy settled in the pit of his stomach. Because if Stu Dorfman was calling, it was because he'd discovered something about Rosie. And for the first time in two weeks, Sam honestly wasn't sure he wanted to know what it was. Mostly because he feared it would be the perfect antidote to counter his terminal happiness problem.

He remembered then that he was supposed to have asked Rosie about her mysterious past himself. That he had, as recently as a couple of days ago, decided to simply confront her with the discrepancies he'd discovered and ask her what they meant. He'd felt as though the two of them had reached a point in their—he might as well admit it—relationship that he could do so without fear of damaging it. So why hadn't he? Why had he instead pushed his decision to do so to the very back of his brain, where it lay neglected and forgotten?

Because he didn't care, he realized. He didn't care who or what Rosie was before she came to Northaven. He didn't care about where she'd come from or where she'd been. He didn't care about what experiences she might have had or how they might have shaped her. Not because he didn't care about her. Quite the contrary as a matter of fact. Nothing she could have done or been would make him care for her any less than he did. All that mattered was what Rosie was now. Who she was now. What she'd done and been since she came into his life. And what she'd been was his salvation.

Maybe that sounded melodramatic, but it was the truth. Since the two of them had gotten involved, Sam had felt better than he'd ever felt in his life. He'd stopped looking for the worst in people and started seeing the best instead. He'd stopped feeling lousy and started feeling happy. He'd stopped giving up and started to feel hope. He'd stopped living in the past and started enjoying his present. Hell, he was even beginning to look forward to—

A light went on inside him that sent warmth seeping throughout his entire body, pooling around his heart. The future. He was beginning to look forward to the future. With Rosie. In Northaven. Which could only mean one thing.

Maybe, on some level, Sam really did think he deserved to be happy. Maybe, on some level, he really had forgiven himself for failing so horribly in Boston. Maybe, on some level, he was thinking it was time to move on. To better things. With someone who made him a better person. Where they could have a better life—together.

It was too much to think about right now. He might not ever understand it entirely. Later, he promised himself as he picked up the phone. Later, he'd think more about it. And he'd talk to Rosie about it. In fact, the two of them had a lot to talk about. And not just because of what Sam might be about to learn from Stu.

Later, he told himself again as he punched the button that would connect him to Miami. There would be time to sort it out later. Because if Sam had anything to say about it, he and Rosie would have all the time in the world.

Steeling himself for whatever Stu had to tell him—not that it would make any difference in how Sam felt about Rosie—he picked up the phone. "Stu," he said in greeting. "What's up?"

"I've been working on your girl," the other detective said without preamble.

Wow, what a coincidence, Sam thought. So had he. But he bet Stu hadn't come to the same staggering conclusions Sam had.

"I had her photo tacked up in the squad room," the other man continued, "just to see if anyone recognized her. I didn't get any leads on her status as a suspect, but—"

"She's not a suspect, Stu," Sam interjected. "She's

someone I wanted to know more about." And, of course, he now knew more about her than he'd ever realized he would. Even more significant, he now knew more about himself than he'd ever realized he would.

"Right," Stu said in that tone of voice every cop recognized as meaning, *Oh, sure…whatever.* "Anyway," the other man continued, "I finally got lucky last night."

Wow, what a coincidence, Sam thought. So had he. And not just because he'd had great sex, either. But because it had been with a woman he loved.

"I brought in a guy from one of the South Beach gangs on a D and D," Stu went on, "and the whole time I was entering his info, he was looking at your girl's picture. I figured at first it was only because, you know, she's an incredibly hot babe."

Sam winced at the terminology, even though it was the kind of thing he might have said himself once upon a time. Back when he'd thought all women were pretty much alike, and that all were interchangeable. Back before he met Rosie and realized how wrong about that he was.

"Anyway, I finally said something to the perp like, 'Yeah, you wish you'd meet a woman like that,' and he said, 'Shows how much you know. I already met her.'"

Sam was shaking his head before Stu finished talking, even though the other man couldn't see what he was doing. "That's impossible, Stu," he said. "Rosie's not the kind of woman who'd be associating with South Beach gangs."

"Yeah, well, I didn't know that, did I? Since you only told me you were interested in her and wanted any info we might have on her. So I let the guy talk. And what he said *was* very interesting, and led to some further investigation on my part, and I just now e-mailed you a photo you might find interesting, too."

"Stu, it's impos—"

"Just trust me on this one, okay? Check it out."

Even though Sam knew it was pointless to continue the conversation, he let Stu talk. He even strode over to the computer to download his e-mail, and clicked on the attachment icon next to the one from Stu.

Stu kept talking as the picture began to download, continuing his story about the South Beach gang member. "He said her name was Lauren Nelson, and that she dated some cokehead client of his a long time ago. He said she was a sweet, young thing then, Goth girl barely out of high school. He was pretty sure she was a snorter, too, and he said she was sleeping with the guy, even though he was old enough to be her father."

Oh, now Sam really knew the perp was full of it. No way did that description fit Rosie.

Just as the thought formed, however, the photo Stu sent appeared in all its glory on the computer screen. And although it didn't look like the Rosie Sam knew, if it wasn't her in the photo, it was for sure her evil twin. Worse, the photo was a mug shot. She'd been arrested for something once upon a time.

"I attached her rap sheet, too," Stu added. "It's in a separate e-mail. Had to get a judge to sign for it, because she was in juvey at the time."

While he waited, Sam sat down at the computer and studied the photo of Rosie—hard. If she was still a teenager when it was taken, that would make it about fifteen years old. Her hair was cropped short, dyed black, and heavy black eyeliner encircled her eyes. Her lipstick, too, was black, as were the ragged fingernails holding the numbered plate in front of herself. Her ears sported a good dozen earrings, and at least that many black rubber bracelets wrapped her wrist.

She looked like dozens of kids he'd seen in the same position—angry, defiant, terrified. But there was still something there that Sam recognized as uniquely Rosie. And that was what assured him the girl in the photo was indeed her.

He downloaded her rap sheet, too, and quickly scanned it. Most of her crimes had consisted of petty theft and vandalism. Probably shoplifted a lot. There was nothing drug-related and there were no prostitution charges, he was relieved to see. Not that that would have changed his feelings for her, but he hated to think about her having to live that life. Though Stu had said the perp he arrested thought Rosie—then Lauren—had been using. And she had been sexually involved with a much older man. Probably some scumbag son of a bitch who had no qualms about using a child. That, in itself, was bad enough.

"She was a runaway starting at the age of thirteen," Stu said. "Every time they sent her home, she took off again. I'll send her social services record through, too. Not as bad as some, but not great. Father unknown, mother was a junkie. Lauren was neglected, but not abused. She finally just started floating from one friend's house to another's. Never graduated from high school."

Sam couldn't jibe the Rosie he knew with the

teenager Stu described. How could a kid have a life like that and grow up to be, not just a functioning member of society, but a woman who was decent, passionate and loving?

Because he knew Rosie must love him, too. Even if she'd never told him so, she'd shown him in a hundred different ways. The same ways, he realized now, that he'd been showing her he loved her. It took a remarkable person to survive what Stu was describing. That Rosie had not only survived, but thrived, meant she was a very special person indeed.

But then, Sam already knew that. It was one of the reasons he loved her.

"There's something else you should know, Sam," Stu said from the other end of the line, bringing Sam's thoughts back to the present. "After the perp ID'd your girl, I ran a check on Lauren Nelson to see if there were any outstanding warrants. And what I discovered was that Lauren Nelson disappeared without a trace almost immediately after appearing as a star witness in a federal trial here in Miami. Guy she'd been sleeping with tried to have a cop killed."

"What?" Sam asked incredulously.

"Even with her testimony, though," Stu continued, "the guy—local businessman named Carl Lorrimer— kicked the rap. Walked away scot-free. Musta cost him a bundle, all the people he had to pay off to do it. But he still wanted her whacked for ratting him out. He put out the word right after the trial fourteen years ago, and then, poof. Suddenly Lauren Nelson doesn't show up anywhere ever again."

"Whoa, whoa, whoa," Sam said, his head spinning as he tried to absorb and digest and make sense of everything Stu was telling him. "What are you saying? That the girl in this photo *isn't* Rosie Bliss? That she got whacked and Rosie took over her identity?"

"No, I'm not sayin' she died," Stu told him.

"But you just told me—"

"I said she disappeared. But that wasn't the most interesting thing," Stu added before Sam could comment.

Someone purported to be dead turned up alive in another state a decade and a half later, and that wasn't the most interesting thing? Sam thought. Just how bad were things down in Miami these days?

"What was most interesting," the other man continued, "was that her page in the system came up flagged by the feds."

Sam narrowed his eyes at that. If the feds had flagged her…

"Then, late yesterday afternoon," Stu went on, "I had a visit from a federal marshal."

Any question Sam might have asked was answered by that little tidbit of information. "Witness protection?" he said.

"Well, the guy didn't confirm it," Stu replied. "They never do. But if one was a reasonably intelligent cop, one could put federal marshal and disappearing witness together and come up with that as an answer, yeah."

Witness protection, Sam repeated to himself. It would explain a lot. Hell, it would explain everything. "So what'd you tell the marshal?" he asked Stu.

"I told him she was a person of interest in another case, but that I didn't have an address for her. Sorry."

"Did he believe you?"

"What else was he gonna do?"

Good question, Sam thought. He just wished he knew the answer to that. Well, that, and a host of other questions besides.

9

EXCEPT FOR THE OCCASIONAL floral delivery—which there weren't an abundance of in a town the size of Northaven—Rosie wasn't accustomed to making house calls for her job. Certainly she'd never had cause to do it for her aphrodisiacs, since her customers always came into the shop to buy those. But midterm week this year was evidently stressing out *a lot* of the college crowd, because she'd received *a lot* of orders for aphrodisiacs over the past week from the college crowd. All from students who offered to pay extra for delivery, since they couldn't even take time from their studies to make the trip into town.

So after coming to terms that morning with her newly discovered feelings for Sam—well, as much as one *could* come to terms with the discovery that one was head over heels in love for the first time in one's life, with a man who might bolt from one's life any minute—Rosie packed up a dozen orders and made the twenty-minute drive to Northaven College.

It was a postcard-perfect campus, especially now, as October drew to a close. Rolling hills spilled to the horizon like great green bumps beneath the bright blue bowl of the sky, dotted here and there with copses of trees stained orange and scarlet and amber. The tiny college lay nestled at their base, a dozen or so brick Georgian structures twined with ages-old ivy and fronted by stout white pillars. Scores of students scurried from one structure to another, their jackets and sweaters a myriad of swirling colors. Here and there, groups sat beneath trees confabbing, and a solitary figure studied a fat tome at the edge of a brook. Rosie noted one overly amorous couple who'd forsaken their studies to share a long kiss in the grass, thinking with a smile that obviously neither was a client.

She inhaled deeply of the crisp autumn air and closed her eyes, holding her breath for as long as she dared. It was a perfect moment, she thought. A moment when all seemed right with the world, and worries seemed packed away forever. She wanted to savor it, even if it only lasted a moment. Life offered so few of them, after all.

When she opened her eyes, the scene was unaltered, and something about that made happiness blossom inside her. Maybe, she thought, things with Sam would work out. Maybe he loved her the same way she loved him. Maybe there was hope for the two of them yet.

Later, she thought. The two of them could talk about that later. After the workday ended and their time together began. She grinned. Really, their time together had begun weeks ago. Their time together never ended. Even when they were separated physically, there was a part of Sam that stayed with her. A part of him that would always be with her. No matter what the future might hold.

Rosie pushed the thought away for now and made her way to the girls' dorms. She'd tucked all the plastic zippered bags into the little fabric pouches she used for more aesthetically pleasing presentation and tagged each with the name of its proper recipient. Then she'd dumped them into an oversize leather satchel along with a sheet of paper onto which she'd recorded each of the girls' names and corresponding dorm numbers.

Now as she strode across campus, Rosie slung the satchel over her shoulder so that it slanted across the slouchy red sweater she wore with a pair of embroidered, bejeweled jeans. Wearing hiking boots, and with her hair woven into a loose braid that fell between her shoulder blades, she could have passed for one of the students herself, she thought. As she made her way toward Bayard Hall, she found herself thinking she should enroll for the spring semester. Maybe get a degree in botany or horticulture or something to go with the business degree she earned at CU Boulder five years ago.

She halted the minute the thought formed in her head. She was making plans for the future, she realized. Plans for a future in Northaven, no less. It had been a long time since she'd allowed herself to think that far ahead. About anything. But it had happened so easily. So naturally. As if her mind were finally allowing her to think in terms of permanence. She just wondered if there was some way she could include others—or, at least one other— in those plans.

She wondered if Sam loved her, too.

She knew he felt something for her. He must. No one could make love to her the way he did and not have some kind of affection attached to it. But was what he felt a deep, long-lasting love for her as a person that would weather the test of time? Or was it just a temporary infatuation with a sexy fling that he'd flunk come midterms? She supposed she would just have to wait and see. And she tried not to feel too disconsolate about honestly not knowing.

As she passed one of the little golf carts used by campus security to patrol the college grounds, Rosie lifted a hand in greeting to Ed Dinwiddie, who was driving it. Ed was kind of odd, frustrated as he was by the lack of crime in their tiny community, but Rosie liked him. She understood what it was to want to be something you feared you'd never be able to be. In Ed's case, it was Dirty Harry. In Rosie's case, it had been downright happy.

But she was downright happy these days, even not knowing exactly how Sam felt about her. So maybe someday Ed would find what he wanted, too. Maybe someday he'd be instrumental in cracking a tough case for the authorities, and then he could write his memoirs and go on a book tour and talk about how he'd dedicated his life to fighting crime. She grinned as she pictured Ed in a deerstalker, smoking an elaborate pipe, even though he was more likely to don riot gear and a big ol' smoking gun.

In fact, even with her confusion about Sam, Rosie was in such a good mood today, she hoped everyone in the world found their bliss. Her grin broadened when she realized her phraseology. She'd deliberately chosen the name Bliss for herself when she started over in

Northaven. And Rosie, too. Even when the marshals told her that wasn't protocol for people in WITSEC to choose their own names, she'd insisted. She'd been so determined that things wouldn't go sour here, the way they had in Boulder, and then Miami before that. Her bliss was definitely here in Northaven. And it was very rosy indeed.

She stopped at the reception desk in the lobby of Bayard Hall to sign in, and once the girl manning the desk had cleared Rosie with three of the students for whom she was making deliveries, she ascended the stairs to the second floor. After exchanging goods for cash, she headed to the next dorm on her list. After that was a student in Darien Hall—Rachel Preston—and once that delivery was made, Rosie could head back to the shop.

Like the other dorms before it, Darien Hall looked more like a manor house than a dormitory, even though it had been built for that purpose nearly a hundred-and-fifty years ago. The third floor, which Rachel called home, was spotlessly clean, its hardwood floor and natural wood trim buffed to a honeyed sheen. A long, claret-colored carpet rolled from one end of the hall to the other beneath walls painted sage green, and antique brass-and-milk-glass light fixtures hung at regular intervals from the ceiling. The room numbers were brass, as well, as bright and polished as the rest of the place, and the faint aroma of lemon oil drifted pleasantly through the air.

Rachel, on the other hand, looked ready to spit nails when she opened the door to Rosie's knocking, the rigors of midterms obviously having taken their toll. Her curly blond hair danced wildly about her face as if it hadn't been brushed for a week, and faint purple crescents smudged her eyes. Her plaid flannel shirt was untucked over jeans that were more rip than denim, and the buttons weren't aligned properly. Her entire posture was rigid and tense, but she immediately relaxed when she saw that it was Rosie at the door.

"Oh, thank God you're here," Rachel said, punctuating the sentiment with a dramatic sigh. "If I had to go one more day without it, I was going kill someone. Probably Michael. You did bring it, right? You brought the stuff?"

Somehow Rosie refrained from rolling her eyes. "Yes, Rachel, I brought the stuff."

"Great. I've got your money. Hang on."

As Rachel retreated into her dorm, Rosie fished the last of the fabric pouches from her satchel and waited for the young woman's return. As had happened a couple of weeks ago in Alice's aerobics studio, she suddenly got the feeling she was being watched, and she jerked her head quickly to the side to see if anyone was there. But the hall was empty and tranquil, so she shook the sensation off almost literally.

Rachel returned then with a fistful of wrinkled bills and thrust them at Rosie with one hand while she opened the other palm up. "Gimme," she said. "I gotta have it. Now. Michael's on his way over."

Rosie accepted the money and dropped the pouch into Rachel's hand, but before the young woman had even closed her fingers over it, a voice called out from behind her, "Freeze!"

When Rosie turned this time, the hall wasn't empty at all. It was filled with Ed Dinwiddie, which, she supposed, explained why she'd had the feeling she was being watched. It didn't, however, explain why he was pointing a gun at her.

But before she could say something—something like, "Ed, this is no way to find your bliss"—he was yelling again, this time crying, "Hold it right there! Keep your hands where I can see 'em! Both of you!"

For a moment, neither Rosie nor Rachel said a word, only stood in the latter's doorway gazing at Ed in dumfounded disbelief. Then Rachel dropped her hands to her hips and shifted all her weight to one foot, glaring.

"Ed, what the hell do you think you're doing?" she demanded. "Remember what happened the last time you drew your weapon. Dean Foster barred you from all future sorority bake sales and you immediately went into lemon bar withdrawal. For God's sake, put that thing away."

For a moment, Ed looked a little panicked, the gun in his hand drooping a bit. But he quickly regrouped and tightened his hold, pointing the weapon fiercely at the two women again. "Don't mess with me, missy," he told Rachel. "Drop the dope."

Rosie looked at Rachel, who looked back at her, seeming every bit as confused. Then they both looked back at Ed.

"Drop the dope?" they chorused

"In your hand," Ed said, ducking his head at Rachel's curled fingers. "Drop it. Now. I mean it."

As one, Rachel and Rosie both looked at the little

fabric pouch. As one, they looked at each other. And then, as one, they both burst out laughing.

"Ed!" Rachel managed to cry through her laughter. "This isn't dope. It's—"

"Potpourri," Rosie quickly interjected, thinking that would be a lot easier to explain to Ed than an aphrodisiac would.

But Ed wasn't buying it. "Drop it," he said again. "And keep your hands where I can see them."

With a sigh of unmistakable regret, Rachel rolled her eyes at Rosie and did as he instructed, tossing the pouch to the floor. With his gun still trained on them both, Ed inched his way up the hall and, with an agility that his girth belied, bent to sweep it up in his palm. He fumbled one-handed with the little drawstring until he had it opened, then he withdrew the plastic bag from inside.

Once again, Rosie was struck by how much the herbal blend resembled marijuana, and dread filled her when she realized she wasn't the only one who thought that. Because Ed looked up from the bag in his hands with clear disgust for her and Rachel both.

"Drugs," he spat. "On my campus. You two should be ashamed of yourselves."

"It's not drugs, Ed," Rosie said earnestly. "It's—"

But he interrupted her before she finished, clearly not believing a word of what she said. "I knew it," he muttered, his gaze ricocheting from Rosie to Rachel and back again. "I knew it all along. I knew you were selling drugs on campus. And now I have the proof."

"Ed, please," Rosie tried again. "That's not what you think it is. It's an herbal tea blend." And then the rest of his statement hit her, and she was filled with more righteous indignation than he was displaying himself. "Wait a minute. You've been thinking all along that I was selling drugs? *Me?* Are you serious? Ed! How could you?"

In response, he waved the bag of tea at her, then quickly jerked it back again, as if he feared she might grab it and swallow it, eliminating all traces of evidence. And also choking herself to death in the process, since the bag was big enough to choke a yak.

"It's tea, Ed," she said again. "I make it myself in the shop."

"You just said it was potpourri," he reminded her.

So she had. "Yeah, well, it can be potpourri or tea. That's the beauty of it."

"It's neither," Ed countered. "It's a controlled substance."

"Actually," Rachel interjected with a grin, "it's a substance that makes you totally lose control. You should try it, Ed. Trust me, if anyone needs it, you do."

He huffed out his disapproval. "Unlike some people, I can just say no. You're under arrest. Both of you. For trafficking in narcotics. Now come along peacefully."

Rosie couldn't believe her ears. Arrested? For selling tea? "Ed," she said, doing her best to keep her voice level. "Open the bag. Smell what's inside. Marijuana does *not* have a hint of cinnamon and the slightest suggestion of mint."

He shook his head. "No way. We'll let the crime lab sort out what you put in with the dope to disguise it. Right now, you're both coming with me."

As he concluded the order, two other campus cops

appeared from the stairwell at the end of the hall, both younger versions of Ed, right down to their crew cuts and drawn guns. But then, how else were they supposed to protect themselves and society from all the dangerous, tea-toting mamas on the lam? Rosie could whip out an infuser any minute and brew them all to death. The two women exchanged disbelieving looks, then, both understanding they didn't have much choice in the matter, lifted their hands chest high. The other two security guards came forward to relieve them of the money in Rosie's hand, her satchel and the list of names poking out of her blue jeans pocket.

It occurred to her then that she'd just potentially, however inadvertently, tied every one of her customers to a nonexistent crime, and that Ed was going to round up all the students on that list after he took Rosie and Rachel to the campus security office. She knew a simple test of the tea would prove it was exactly what she said it was, but who knew how long it would take for that test to be performed and the results to come in? In the meantime, would Ed ransack the shop and find the rest of her blends? Would he search her sales records and discover who her other customers were? What would the mayor say when Ed knocked on her door, handcuffs at the ready, and arrested her, too?

Even after Rosie and her clientele were exonerated, there could still be trouble. Although aphrodisiacs were by no means illegal, there was nevertheless a sort of stigma attached to them in contemporary American society. They were sexual products, and a lot of people got wiggy about sex outside the bedroom. Hell, a lot of people got wiggy about sex *inside* their bedrooms, poor things. Rosie wouldn't be bothered by the talk that was sure to follow her "outing," but some of her customers might. Like the aforementioned mayor. And the head of the chamber of commerce. And Mrs. Doheny, the first-grade teacher at Northaven Elementary.

And then, if the press got wind of it, which it inevitably would—

Oh, God, Rosie thought. The press. Every day in Northaven was a slow news day. Something like this would make the front page of the daily *Northaven Monitor.* Her picture might even show up in the paper. And this was just the sort of cute, fluffy, human-interest story that would make it to the network news shows. She could already hear Katie Couric's voice: "Remember that slogan, Say It With Flowers? Well, now you can talk dirty with flowers, too."

It would be Boulder all over again, Rosie thought. Things had gone to hell there when her retail business flourished to the point where she'd received national coverage for it. Her photo had appeared in a trade magazine, and she'd been recognized by one of Carl Lorrimer's cronies as the woman who'd nearly put him behind bars. Then Carl had sent someone to Boulder to try and kill her.

If her arrest today were publicized, if her picture even made it into local papers, the same thing could happen again here in Northaven. Just as she had in Boulder, and earlier in Miami, Rosie would have to disappear without a trace. She wouldn't have time to pack or tell anyone goodbye. She'd have to leave everything behind and move thousands of miles away and start all

over, severing ties to everything she'd come to love.
And to everyone.

She was going to have to leave Northaven, she
thought as sick dread filled her stomach.

She was going to have to leave Sam.

WHEN SAM GOT THE CALL from Ed Dinwiddie saying
he'd just broken the campus drug case wide open, he
expected the worst. Ed breaking wind was disastrous
enough. Sam couldn't imagine the repercussions of the
man actually making an arrest. But even after trying to
prepare himself, he was stunned by what greeted him
when he arrived at Campus Security office.

Women in chains. The manifestation of every Eisen-
hower-era adolescent boy's wet dreams. The reality of
a fantasy that had driven the entire Hollywood genre of
women-in-prison films. Because there in the campus
security office stood a line of a good dozen women, one
handcuffed to the other, with the final cuff locked tight
around a radiator in the corner. The women came in all
shapes and sizes and colors, and appeared in various
stages of dress—and undress. Everything from sweat-
shirts and pajama bottoms to dangerously dipping blue
jeans and cropped sweaters. A couple wore only skimpy
boxers and tiny T-shirts.

And just like that, Sam knew how Ed Dinwiddie had
spent most of his afternoons as a boy. He also understood then just how badly he'd underestimated the
power of Ed. Especially when he saw that one of the
women in chains was none other than Rosie Bliss. That,
more than anything else, really pissed Sam off.

As he strode up to Ed's desk, he tried very hard to control his impatience. And he tried even harder to control his fist. The first stayed pretty well simmering below the surface. The last, however, wanted very, very badly to plant itself in the other man's nose.

"Ed," Sam managed through gritted teeth as he flattened his palms on the desk and bent down to get in the other man's face, "just what the *hell* do you think you're doing?" Okay, so maybe the impatience wasn't simmering *that* far below the surface.

Ed had been typing furiously on his computer—though whether it was his crime report or notes for his blockbuster memoir, Sam couldn't have said—but looked up triumphantly at Sam's question. Then he stood and hitched up his belt, fairly bursting the buttons of his shirt with his pride at having done such an excellent job, ridding the world of dangerous coeds. Well, that, and having consumed the contents of the Pablo's Pizza Padua box now sitting empty on his desk.

"Busted the dealer and twelve users," Ed said smugly. "It's a banner day for campus security. I told you Rosie Bliss was trafficking on campus."

Sam nodded. "I see. And what the *hell* kind of evidence do you have to support your arrests?"

Ed jutted a thumb over his shoulder at a table situated behind his desk, where sat a dozen small plastic bags filled with something brown and dried and botanical. Alongside them was an envelope full of money and a ball of wadded-up cash.

"I witnessed the exchanges myself," Ed said, hooking his hands back into the waistband of his uniform trousers. He nodded toward the motley group on the other side of the room. "Rosie Bliss gave each of those women a bag of pot, and each of those women gave her money in return. That big wad of dead presidents," he added, making Sam wince at the injection of outdated street slang, "came from Rachel Preston. I took it from her hands myself. But I'm sure your guys can lift prints from some of the other bills."

Right, Sam thought. He'd have the CSI: Northaven team get right on it.

"They were bona fide drug transactions," Ed said emphatically. He made a V with two fingers and pointed at his eyes. "And I saw it all happen with my own two peepers. Right there in the dorms. I was waiting for you to get here before I organized the press conference." He lowered his voice and dipped his head to Sam's conspiratorily. "Truth be told, Sam, I'm not sure how to go about organizing one of those. I could use some tips."

Oh, boy, Sam thought. A little knowledge really was a dangerous thing. He shifted his weight to one foot, hooked his hands on his own hips, and wondered how to tell Ed politely that he was a great, hulking idiot. Finally, he met the other man's gaze levelly and said, "Well, here's my first tip, Ed. Next time you arrest people for buying and selling drugs, you might want to make sure it's drugs that the people are buying and selling."

Ed's bushy brows drew downward. "Whattaya mean?"

Now Sam was the one who pointed at the plastic bags. "I mean that's not pot," he said with absolute conviction. "I don't know what it is, but it isn't marijuana."

Ed's mouth dropped open. "Of course it's marijuana."

Instead of replying, Sam moved around the desk and reached for the wad of bills Ed had lifted from Rachel. One by one, he smoothed them flat. There were ten of them. All ones. He dipped his head again toward the plastic bags full of…whatever was in them. "You say Rachel used this money to buy one of those bags from Rosie?"

"Yep," Ed confirmed. He did the V thing with his fingers again and again pointed at his eyes. "Saw it with my own two—"

"This is the entire amount Rachel turned over?"

Ed nodded. V at the eyes. "Like I said. Saw it with—"

"Ten dollars, Ed," Sam interrupted again. "A bag of pot the size of these would go for at least five times that amount on the street."

"But—"

"Not to mention I've cataloged enough cannabis in my career to recognize it when I see it. And this ain't it, Ed. Trust me."

"But—"

"Now uncuff all those women and let's get this sorted out."

Although, Sam thought as he looked over at Rosie again, he kind of liked the thought of cuffing her himself later. He wondered why they hadn't tried that already?

Then he remembered that the woman cuffed to Ed's radiator might not be the woman to whom Sam had thought he was making love for the past two weeks. She might not be the woman with whom he'd fallen in love over the past two weeks. She might be someone else entirely. Everything about her—her name, her occupation, her past, her life—wasn't what he'd thought it was. *She* wasn't what—or who—he'd thought she was.

He wasn't bothered so much by her having kept secrets. Everyone was entitled to have those. And he and Rosie hadn't exactly pledged their undying devotion for all time to each other, so neither of them had owed the other any explanations or revelations. What bothered Sam was that he might not know Rosie as well as he'd been thinking he knew her. With everything Stu had told him, she had suddenly become someone else. And where Sam had thought Rosie Bliss might be falling in love with him the way he'd been falling in love with her, he had no idea what this other woman might do.

He still loved Rosie. Nothing would ever change that. But he felt a little weird inside right now. He'd come to Northaven so he wouldn't have to be afraid of losing anything ever again. And now—

Now he was afraid he might be losing everything.

"Aphrodisiacs," Sam said after Rosie concluded her explanation.

It had taken her all of fifteen minutes to plead her case for exoneration and prove what she said was true— mainly by boiling a kettle of water on Ed's hot plate and brewing up a scoop of the not-so-controlled substance in one of the bags. Sam, of course, had already known the product wasn't marijuana. Although it did bear a passing resemblance to cannabis, God knew he'd seen enough of it in his time to recognize it without having to perform a lab test. Ed still hadn't been convinced, however, even when the tea, redolent of cinnamon and mint, turned out to obviously be tea. So one of the Northaven students in the skimpy sleepwear had hauled out a rolling paper, deftly prepared a tea joint, and lit it. The smell was atrocious. And clearly *not* pot.

"You're not supposed to smoke it, Becca," Rosie said now as the young woman with the cropped black hair and enormous blue eyes enjoyed another puff.

"It's not illegal," Becca said. "And smoking it works even better than brewing it."

This was obviously news to Rosie, whose mouth dropped open in surprise. "It does?"

Becca nodded. "And there are no ill effects to the lungs if it's only occasionally," she added. "I asked my dad. He's a pulmonologist."

"You told your father you're smoking aphrodisiacs?" Rosie asked incredulously.

Becca shrugged. "Sure. Half the stuff I buy is for him and my mom. Though they prefer to bake it into brownies."

Rosie seemed to give that some thought, then said, "Oh. Um, do you think she'd give me her recipe?"

"Probably. I'll ask her. She said something about entering them in the South Dakota State Fair this summer." Becca enjoyed another puff and looked at Ed. "Are we finished here, Ed?" she asked. "Because smoking this stuff always makes it work way faster than drinking it, and I'd just as soon find Chuck before it starts to take effect."

Ed looked at Sam, who nodded that whoa, yeah, they were beyond finished here.

"You can go, Becca," Ed said reluctantly. But Becca

was off to look for Chuck before he even finished talking. Clearly devastated by the lack of crime on campus, Ed, sounding like a three-year-old who'd been denied his favorite Power Ranger, added, "All of you can go. I'm sorry for the inconvenience."

One by one, the remaining students filed out of the room. All but Rachel, who gestured to the bag of herbs on Ed's desk. "Can I have that back now?" she asked. "I, um, sorta have plans later." When Ed nodded, she swept up what was left of the tea and hastened from the room.

Looked like it was going to be a busy night at North-aven College, Sam thought. Gonna be a whole lotta boinkin' goin' on. He glanced over at Rosie. Too bad he couldn't say the same thing for the two of them. They had too much talking to do first.

"Can I give you a lift back to town?" he asked her.

She shook her head. "I have my car."

"Then you can follow me," he said.

"To the station?"

Sam shook his head. "To my house. We need to talk."

10

TALK, ROSIE REPEATED to herself a half hour later as she sat at Sam's kitchen table staring back at him. Funny, but they'd been at his house for a full five minutes and hadn't spoken a single word to each other. He'd gone straight to his refrigerator and withdrawn a longneck from the door, gesturing a silent question as to whether or not she wanted one herself. She'd shaken her head in a silent reply. Only the beer had offered commentary on the situation, by hissing as Sam twisted off its cap. If one of them didn't say something soon, Rosie was going to start hissing herself.

As if he'd read her mind, Sam finally opened his mouth to speak. But she was totally unprepared for the words that came out of his mouth. "Tell me about Lauren Nelson," he said.

Heat exploded in her belly and burned in her chest, spreading like wildfire to her neck, face and hands. It was a name Rosie hadn't heard spoken in years. And it belonged to a person she hadn't been in contact with for more than a decade. Weird, since Lauren Nelson was someone she'd known intimately all her life.

"H-how did you find out about Lauren Nelson?" she asked.

Sam hesitated a moment before replying, "I'm a cop, Rosie. Finding out stuff is what I do."

She nodded. "And what made you go looking for Lauren in the first place?"

He blew out a long sigh, but his gaze never once left hers. "It wasn't so much that I went looking for her specifically," he finally said. "She turned up when I went looking for you."

Another flash of heat seared Rosie's midsection at his remark. "And what made you go looking for me?" she asked carefully. "I mean, I've been right here under your nose for a year."

Sam sighed again, with much less gusto and a little more fatigue. "Ed," he said simply. "Ed Dinwiddie did. He was so convinced you were selling drugs on campus that he was on the verge of starting an investigation of his own. I was afraid that, at best, he'd end up making a nuisance of himself and, at worst, he might skirt harassment behavior. So I told him I'd look into it. Why didn't you just tell me you were hawking aphrodisiacs?" he added. "Hell, Rosie, why don't you advertise it? I mean, it sounds like it's a significant part of your business."

She was grateful for the change of subject, since it allowed her a little more time to gather her thoughts together about Lauren. Somehow, she suspected Sam had done it on purpose, and she was grateful for that, too.

"I didn't tell you at first," she said, "because I wasn't sure how you'd react to the whole aphrodisiac thing. I was afraid you'd think I was a flake. And then I didn't tell you because—"

She halted abruptly, unsure how to tell him he'd inadvertently consumed her aphrodisiac tea that morning in her shop, and how his attraction to her had almost certainly been accelerated by doing so. Had he not been so turned-on that morning—and she knew he had been as turned-on as she—he might never have agreed to go out with her. And if he hadn't gone out with her, they might never have gotten together the way they had.

Even as the thoughts unfolded in her head, however, Rosie knew the explanation was inadequate. Maybe—maybe—having drunk the tea had speeded things up between her and Sam. But she'd been attracted to him from the moment she met him, and there hadn't been any tea in sight that day. And she'd seen him giving her enough longing looks over the past year to know he was at least a little interested in her. She was confident they would have hooked up eventually. At least, if she'd had anything to say about it. Still, he deserved to know that he'd been under the influence that day in her shop.

"And then I didn't tell you because—" she began again, picking up where she'd left off her last sentence "—because you'd accidentally dosed yourself with one of my aphrodisiacs, and I was afraid of what would happen if you found out."

He studied her curiously. "What are you talking about?"

This time Rosie was the one to draw a deep breath and release it. "You remember that morning in my shop when I asked you out?" she began.

He nodded. "Of course."

"Remember that tea you poured yourself to drink?"

He nodded again, more slowly than before.

"That tea I tried to stop you from drinking?"

This time, there was only one nod. And a very troubled expression.

"It wasn't just herbal tea," she told him.

No nod at all. Very troubled expression indeed.

Rosie made herself push the words out of her mouth, and they came with the speed and precision of a sub-atomic warhead. "It was a new aphrodisiac blend I was testing, and I'd just had a cup myself and was waiting for it to take effect, then you walked into the shop and had some, too, and it worked a lot more quickly than I thought it would, and that's why the two of us…"

She stopped at that, hoping she'd hit her target well enough that Sam would be able to draw any necessary conclusions himself—without there being so much fallout that their feelings would have to survive a nuclear winter before they had any hope of regenerating the human race.

Her hopes were dashed when he spurred her, "And that's why the two of us…what?"

Not wanting to see his reaction, she closed her eyes as she finished, "That's why the two of us responded so strongly to each other that morning. It's why you agreed to go out with me even after telling me you were busy the first time I asked."

When Sam said nothing in reply, Rosie hopefully opened her eyes again. His expression hadn't changed at all, but a muscle twitched in his jaw. She tried to reassure herself that it bore no resemblance whatsoever to a mushroom cloud on the horizon. But it still looked a little ominous.

"You think that's why I agreed to go out with you?" he said. "Because I was turned-on by something I drank?"

She shook her head. "Well, maybe not entirely. But the aphrodisiac helped. A lot." She sighed again, and told him the rest. "There was an aphrodisiac in the massage oil we used at your house that night, too. That night when we, um, broke our record for number of times we, um, peaked."

Sam shook his head. "You'll never make me believe that some outside substance, some stimulant, is responsible for the way you and I are together."

"I agree with you," Rosie said. "What the two of us have is generated by a fundamental, natural response we have to each other. But the things people consume *can* alter their moods, Sam," she added. "Illegal and legal substances both. Alcohol. Nicotine. Chocolate. Drugs to treat depression and anxiety. For thousands of years people have improved their moods by ingesting things. And just as there are substances that can lift our spirits, there are substances that can trigger our libidos. Those are the ones I use in my teas. And that morning, Sam, I'd just had a cup, and I was definitely feeling…libidinous. Then you came in and…"

"So then you're saying you only asked me out in the first place because you were turned-on that day," he concluded, his voice even flatter than before.

"No," she hurried to tell him. "Sam, you turned me on the day I first met you. More than turned me on. You…" Fearing she would say too much, Rosie halted, then turned to choose a safer route. "If I'd known things were going to turn out the way they did with us…" But she let her voice trail off again, because she was no more certain of this path than she'd been of the other.

Sam, however, immediately picked up her track. "And just how did things turn out with us, Rosie?"

He had to ask? she thought. That wasn't a good sign. Nevertheless, she knew that if there was ever a time to bare her soul, this was it. So, very cautiously, she said, "Well, I can't speak for both of us, but speaking for myself, I…" She swallowed hard and told him the truth. "I…fell in love with you."

He said nothing in reply at first, sending something cold and oily creeping into Rosie's soul. Maybe Sam didn't love her, after all. Although neither of them had said the word, Rosie had recognized the feeling in herself. And once she'd recognized it in herself, she'd started to think there was a good chance Sam felt the same way. He treated her with such tenderness, such sweetness, such affection. The same way she, in her love, treated him. And he seemed so happy when they were together—as happy as she was herself, feeling so much love for him. Had she just been imagining it? Thinking wishfully? Wanting to see love in him because it was there in her? Had she been horribly wrong?

Quietly, tentatively, her gaze never leaving his, she said, "This, um, this might be a good time for you to speak for yourself."

He expelled a single, soft breath. "If you're asking me do I love you…"

"That's what I'm asking," she said.

He continued to study her in silence for another moment, a moment when Rosie felt as if the very earth beneath her was beginning to shift.

Then he nodded. Slowly. Surely. And the world

thumped comfortably back into place. Still, she wanted—needed—to hear him say the words aloud.

"Yeah," he finally told her. "I love you. That was never more obvious than it was today, when I found out what I did about Lauren Nelson—about you," he hastily corrected himself. "I realized there was a chance, however small, that I might lose you. And it scared the hell out of me, Rosie. I'm not a man who scares easily. I'm having trouble getting used to it. But yeah. I do love you. No matter what name you go by."

The tension knotting Rosie's body eased some as he spoke, and she reached across the table to cover his hand with hers. "You don't have to get used to the fear, Sam," she told him. "Because you don't have to feel it. I'm not going anywhere."

And she wasn't, now that everything was straightened out with Ed Dinwiddie and campus security. She could go back to what she had always hoped would be her normal life, in this normal town, with all its normal occurrences. But now there would be one extraordinary exception. Sam would be living it with her.

She hoped.

Although she was greatly encouraged by everything he'd just said, she knew it was a little premature for her to feel complete confidence that all was well. "I guess if we're going to do this thing right," she said, "then we need to be honest with each other about everything, don't we?"

Sam nodded. "Honesty would be good. Full disclosure would be even better."

She nodded, too. It was time, she thought. Past time, really. She'd never thought she would share her past experiences with anyone, because she'd never thought anyone existed who would understand. Or even if she found someone who would understand everything, she'd feared they wouldn't be able to look at her—feel about her—the way they did before hearing about the circumstances of her life. But Sam wasn't just anyone. Which, she supposed, was why she'd fallen in love with him in the first place.

"Then in the interest of full disclosure," she said, "I'll tell you all about Lauren Nelson."

In a way, she hoped, that would make sense to him. She knew if she started at the beginning, they could be here all night, and he probably wouldn't be able to keep track of all the background stuff anyway. Not until she got his attention with the main thing. And that main thing was—

"WITSEC."

Strangely, it wasn't Rosie who said the word. It was Sam.

"Witness Security," he immediately elaborated. "The witness protection program. You're in it."

So he knew about that, too, she thought. And for a moment, the realization terrified her. If Sam knew she was in the program, and where she was now, then others might know it, too. Including Carl Lorrimer. The man who wanted her dead.

"It's okay," Sam said, lifting a hand in a placating gesture, as if he'd read her thoughts. "No one else knows who or where you are now."

"But how?" she asked. "How do *you* know?"

He dropped his gaze to the beer that had been sitting neglected on the table before him when they started talking. As he spoke, he began to worry the label with his thumb, as if he needed to have something to do with his hands. "When I started looking into your background for Ed," he began slowly, deliberately, as if he were choosing every word carefully before speaking it, "I called a few contacts I have in other cities and asked them to see if they could find out anything about you in their records. You'd mentioned that day in your shop that you grew up in the South, so I focused my attentions in that region."

Damn, Rosie thought as she closed her eyes. She'd known even telling him that much could cause her trouble. Hadn't she learned the hard way how important it was that she protect herself?

"Long story short," he continued, bringing her attention back to the conversation, "someone in Miami recognized you from your photo as Lauren Nelson, and I talked to a detective there today who told me about what happened when you were living there."

Fear chilled Rosie to the bone at his words. "What photo?" she asked.

"Your DMV photo," Sam said. "I e-mailed it to the other detectives, and the one in Miami had it displayed in the precinct down there."

"Oh, God," Rosie said, her fear morphing into something much, much worse. "Someone had a new picture of me on display down there? Sam, do you realize what you've done? If anyone down there finds out I'm up here—"

"No one will," he hastily assured her, holding up his hand palm out, as if he could stop the news from spreading that way. "Don't worry, Rosie. Stu, my detective friend down there, hasn't told anyone where your photo came from. He won't tell anyone where you are."

Terror still gripping her, Rosie objected, "But how can I be sure—"

"Cops have a very strong code of ethics," Sam interrupted, "and Stu's one of the best. He wouldn't think of telling anyone he has a lead to your current location, least of all someone who might endanger you." His gaze so intense now it fairly pinned her in place, Sam continued, "Stu's first partner was murdered by a Miami gang. He hates those guys even more than you do. He won't tell anyone, Rosie. I promise. You're safe."

He was so strong in his conviction, she felt herself wavering. Nevertheless, "He's a total stranger," she pointed out. "How can I trust—"

"I was a stranger to you once, too," he reminded her. "And you trust me."

"That's different," she said softly. "I love you."

He stood and moved to the other side of the table, dropped into the chair beside her, and covered both of her hands with his. Slowly, he lifted them to his mouth and brushed his lips over her fingers. He continued to hold them in a way Rosie could only describe as protective as he said, with even more conviction than before, "Then believe me when I tell you you're safe here. You always will be safe here. I promise you that, Rosie. I promise."

She was surprised to discover she believed him. There was just something about Sam, about the way he made her feel, that made her think nothing in her life would ever go wrong again. It wasn't going to be easy, she knew. She would probably always carry the fear of discovery, no matter where she lived or who she was. But she didn't have to live with that fear alone anymore. And somehow, that made her feel almost invincible.

She nodded slowly to let him know she believed him, and, still clasping her hands in his, Sam continued.

"So now that I've heard from Stu how things went down with the Carl Lorrimer case, I'd like to hear your own version of the story."

Rosie would just as soon not have to revisit that chapter of her life, but reminded herself of how Sam had shared his own tragic story of Roni with her—even before he'd fallen in love with her. And something told Rosie that sharing her experiences in Miami with Sam might take away some of the power those events still held over her. Even more significant, she realized she *wanted* to share her experiences in Miami with him. She wanted to share everything with him.

So, "I grew up in Miami," she began, "but I left home for good when I was sixteen. I never knew my father, and my mother was…" She drew a deep breath and expelled it slowly, meeting Sam's gaze levelly. "Well, I imagine you heard from Stu what kind of home life I had as a kid."

Sam nodded, but said nothing more.

So Rosie continued. "For the first six months after I left home, I lived with girlfriends. Kim for a couple of weeks, Danette for a month, Ashley for another month, that kind of thing. But I knew I couldn't keep that up forever. So when one of my friend's fathers offered to put me up in an apartment and give me a monthly allowance in exchange for…" She sighed heavily and closed her eyes. "Well, you can guess what for. And I accepted. He was divorced from her mother," Rosie hastened to add, opening her eyes again to meet Sam's gaze. "But even if he hadn't been…" Her voice trailed off, but she made herself tell the truth, because she knew she had to be honest. "Even if he hadn't been, I would have taken him up on the offer.

"I was seventeen, Sam," she hurried on, dropping her gaze to their entwined hands. "I was a scared, troubled kid. A completely different person from who I am today. And in a weird way, I was kind of in love with him. At least," she qualified, "what I thought at that point in my life was love." She shrugged halfheartedly. "So I let him pay my way, and I gave him what he wanted. I'm certainly not proud of myself and I'm sorry that's the way it was, but there it is all the same."

When Rosie braved a look up at Sam's face, she saw that his jaw had set hard while she was talking, and his eyes had turned icy cold. She thought he was angry because of what she'd told him about herself, and she felt tears stinging her eyes.

Then, his voice filled with steel and venom, he said, "A guy my age or older took advantage of a troubled seventeen-year-old girl in the most heinous way possible, and you're the one apologizing. What's wrong with this picture? If I had five minutes alone with the son of a bitch, I'd show him the kind of trouble he could never imagine."

She nodded, having felt the same way herself a time

or two since those days. "His name was Carl Lorrimer," she continued. "About a year after I got involved with him, he offered me a job, said he'd teach me about his business. I was just kind of his Girl Friday at first, but after a few months, he really did start showing me how his development company ran." She chuckled sadly as more memories hit her. "I honestly started having fantasies about marrying him someday and being a partner in the business. I can't believe how naive I was."

"You were a kid," Sam said quietly. "And he was a manipulative prick. He could have made you believe anything he wanted."

More memories began to tumble into Rosie's head then, one after another, and it took a moment for her to sort through them all. Sam sat patiently as she did, still holding her hands in his, still giving her the strength somehow to work through everything. He was a beacon of goodness and decency amid her dark and dreary recollections. And she knew he would always be there for her, no matter what. So she told him the rest of the story.

"Carl must have assumed he really did have me under his thumb," she said, "because a lot of what he taught me about the business was downright illegal, and he didn't try to hide any of it. Everything from bribing government officials to cooking the books to laundering money for a couple of Miami gangs. But even that wasn't the worst of it."

Although Rosie wouldn't have thought it possible, Sam's eyes went even colder at that, and his mouth flattened into a tight line. He knew what was coming next, she realized. Stu must have already told him.

In spite of that, he asked, "What was the worst of it?"

She swallowed to alleviate the dryness in her mouth, but had no idea what to do about the tightness in her chest. Except try to ease some of it by sharing it with Sam. "The worst," she said, "was when Carl told one of his assistants to murder a cop who was investigating him and getting too close for comfort. Carl gave the order in my presence. I heard him clear as day. That's how sure he was that I was completely under his control. He was that confident he'd get away with it."

Rosie inhaled another deep breath and released it slowly, hoping that might steady her nerves. What had happened in Miami so long ago seemed now as if it had happened to someone else. And she supposed, in a way, it had. Lauren Nelson had been a confused, terrified, troubled kid. Rosie Bliss was none of those things. Not anymore. Never again. And where Lauren had had to go through what she did alone, Rosie would always have Sam to help her deal with whatever life threw at her.

"That was my wake-up call," she said. "I went to the police the minute after I left Carl that night. And I told them everything. I promised to do whatever I had to do to make sure Carl went to jail for a long, long time. Unfortunately, it wasn't just politicians he had in his pocket. He bought off enough people during his trial to walk away without a scratch."

"So as an eighteen-year-old kid," Sam said, "you put yourself in danger to cooperate with authorities, then left everything and everyone you knew to go into hiding. And it was all for nothing."

Immediately, she shook her head. "It wasn't for

nothing. There's a cop in Miami snuggling with his wife and watching his kids grow up because of me. I'd do it all again in a heartbeat to ensure that."

Sam blew out a long breath and lifted a hand to scrub it over his face. "Something tells me there's even more to this story than you've told me so far."

Rosie nodded. "That was just chapter one. You might want to put on a kettle for some tea."

He actually chuckled at that. "Better make it coffee instead."

11

SAM SPENT THE NEXT HOUR listening to the rest of the story of Rosie's life. Not just the part about Miami and Carl Lorrimer, but about what happened after the trial. About how Carl threatened to kill her afterward for turning him in and cooperating with the authorities. About the Miami cops calling in the federal marshals to get her into the Witness Security Program. About how she'd been sent first to live in Colorado as Amanda Drummond, where she'd tested for her GED and enrolled at UC Boulder—and received counseling for all she'd been through.

And he heard about the period after she graduated with a business degree—completing the work in three years instead of the usual four—and how she started to turn her life around. She was hired after graduation to manage a funky shop on Pearl Street Mall that specialized in New Age paraphernalia, literature and attire. It was there that she learned about aphrodisiacs and herbal remedies. When the owner retired a few years later, Rosie, as Amanda, had bought the place from her and, over the next two years, built it into one of the area's most successful shops.

It was so successful, in fact, that she was planning to turn it into a national franchise when the cover for her new identity was blown. Because of her remarkable success, she'd been written about as a fast-rising young retail star in an industry magazine, complete with photos of her and her shop. That was why and how she was discovered living in Boulder. Someone had seen the spread and recognized her, then reported the discovery to Carl Lorrimer.

She'd almost been murdered in Boulder. The guy Lorrimer sent had tried to make it look like an armed robbery of her store, but Rosie and the two college girls who'd been working with her that day had escaped with their lives because an off-duty policewoman had been there shopping at the time and interceded, wounding the gunman before he could hurt anyone. The investigation afterward had revealed that the robber was actually a hired killer, paid by Carl to make good on his promise to kill Rosie.

When Sam heard that part of the story, his first impulse had been to get on a plane, fly down to Miami, hunt down Carl Lorrimer like a dog, and beat him into a coma. Instead, he made a silent vow—to himself and to Rosie—that no one, *no one,* would ever, *ever,* harm her again. She was safe in Northaven. She was safe with him. And as God was his witness, Sam would make sure it stayed that way.

After the attempt on Rosie's life in Boulder, WITSEC entered her life a second time. This time, the marshals moved her to Northaven, where she changed her name again, and bought the local flower shop from its retiring owner. That was why her social security number hadn't turned up anywhere before her appearance here. She'd been assigned a new one when she left Boulder. The third one she'd had in her life. The last one she ever wanted to have. And if Sam had anything to say about it, it would be. Hell, he'd tell Ed Dinwiddie she'd been deposited here by aliens if he had to. And he knew Stu Dorfman in Miami would bury any information he had about her there.

Sam couldn't imagine an eighteen-year-old kid having to go through what Rosie had. A troubled eighteen-year-old kid at that, who'd been knocked around, taken advantage of and mistreated. It was a wonder she wasn't an angry, sullen miscreant. How she'd become such a happy, easygoing person was a testament to her strength and intelligence and good nature. Hell, Sam hadn't been through nearly the rough times Rosie had and he was an angry, sullen miscreant.

But then he realized that wasn't true. Not anymore. Yeah, when he'd left Boston, he'd been all those things. But he hadn't been any of them for a while now. Had it been Northaven, though, or the people of Northaven like Rosie—or had it been Rosie herself—that had changed him? Probably, he thought, it was a combination of all three. But surely it was Rosie who'd contributed the most. It was there in the way she made him think. In the way she made him laugh. In the way she made him look at the world a little more hopefully. It was she who had been the catalyst in allowing Sam to forgive himself for what he'd let happen to Roni. Because he knew Rosie loved him, and a woman like her—who'd been through so much ugliness and hardship and come out a better person because of it all—wouldn't love a man who didn't deserve to be loved for having done the same.

She'd made him feel things he'd never felt for anyone else before, things that made him a better person. And those feelings had only grown stronger this afternoon, as he'd sat here in his kitchen listening to her describe all the things that had brought her here.

"I'm still scared I'll have to leave Northaven," she said in conclusion to her story. And somehow she looked even more miserable saying that than she had when she'd been talking about her time in Miami.

Sam reared his head back in surprise. "What? Why? Rosie, I thought I convinced you that you're safe here."

"I just can't risk someone telling Carl where he can find me now. That detective in Miami—"

"Won't say a word," Sam assured her again. "Lorrimer wanted to kill a cop, Rosie. Do you realize how much cops hate cop killers?"

"I just don't know if I can trust him," she said again, echoing her earlier fear. But there was less conviction in her voice this time. "Even an accidental mention of me by him—"

"It won't happen," Sam said. "If you can't trust Stu, then trust *me*," he added. "I promise you, Rosie, that you will always be safe here. And I promise you that no one will ever hurt you again. Anybody tries, they have to come through me first."

For a moment, Rosie said nothing in response to Sam's reassurance, only studied him in silence as she weighed what he said. Then, very slowly, she smiled.

Because she realized then that she did trust him. And she trusted him because she loved him. The same way she knew he loved her.

"You're going to have to give me some time to get used to it," she said. "I've never trusted anyone before. And I've never loved anyone before, either. I didn't realize until just now how the two go so naturally hand in hand."

Sam smiled as he reached across the table and closed his fingers around hers. "That's not all that goes hand in hand," he said as he lifted her hand to his mouth. Carefully, he uncurled her fingers to expose her palm, then placed a lingering kiss at its center, sending a shiver of something hot and electric through Rosie's entire body.

Oh, how this man excited her. And oh, how much she loved him. Maybe even from the very start. That first day they met, right after he arrived in Northaven. There had just been something about her reaction to him then. And watching him now, as he treated her hand to another tender kiss, that reaction only multiplied. Suddenly, Rosie had a very good idea for those hands. And since Sam was still in his uniform—complete with handcuffs—she didn't see any reason why she shouldn't introduce that into the conversation, too. After all, it went right along with everything else they'd discussed this afternoon.

"You know, it's interesting that we should be talking about love and trust the way we are now," she said, already growing warm at the prospect. She hadn't had so much as a sip of aphrodisiac tea in days, but her body was responding even more quickly—and more thoroughly—than it had the last time she'd tested a new batch. The hot skin, the sweaty palms, the tingly nipples, the dampness between her legs…

Oh, yeah. She definitely had a good idea.

Her growing desire must have tinted her words or voice, because when Sam glanced up from her hand, he looked a little aroused himself. And he hadn't had any tea, either. How about that? Evidently, love was the most powerful aphrodisiac of all. Who knew?

"Interesting in what way?" he asked, his voice sounding a little thicker than it had before.

She grinned her most seductive grin. "Well, there's this thing I've been wanting to try with your handcuffs," she told him.

His smile turned lascivious at that. "Oh, really?"

She nodded again. "Yeah. But I'm such a law-abiding citizen, I can't think of any reason for you to run me in."

"That's okay," Sam told her, his grin growing more salacious. "I can think of lots of reasons—and ways— to run you in. Hell, Rosie, half the things we've tried together must be illegal somewhere."

She chuckled low at that. "Then when," she asked, "are you going to push me up against a wall and tell me to spread 'em?"

He jerked the handcuffs out of his belt and held them up for her inspection. "Rosie Bliss, you're under arrest for inciting a man to commit sexual mayhem. Into the bedroom, sweetheart. Now."

A thrill of something hot and wild crashed through her, and she stood to follow his order. But she took her time as she made her way to the bedroom, undressing as she went, leaving a shoe here, a sock there, her shirt somewhere else and so forth, so that by the time Sam had her up against the wall in his bedroom, she was completely naked. He'd followed her example to some extent, had unbuttoned his shirt and pulled it free of his trousers, which he'd also unfastened. When she looked over her shoulder, she could see his cock pushing against the garment and knew he was already hard for her.

He tossed the cuffs onto the bed for now, then settled his hands on her naked hips. Dipping his mouth close to her ear, he told her, "I'm going to have to frisk you, Ms. Bliss. This body is, after all, a very dangerous weapon. Now keep those hands flat on the wall where I can see them, and spread your legs wide."

She did as he instructed, splaying her fingers and opening her legs, her entire body growing warm in anticipation. First, Sam skimmed both hands down her right leg, slowly, lightly, his fingertips wreaking havoc on her sensitive flesh. He knelt behind her as he descended, then moved from one ankle to the other, pressing his open mouth against her fanny. As he brought both hands back up her left leg, he dragged his lips lightly over the sensitive swells of her bottom, then dipped his fingers deftly between her legs. She was already wet there, so he had no trouble pushing a finger inside her, moving it in and out…in and out…in and out…in and out…as he nibbled and licked her soft skin.

Then he was rising again, skimming his wet finger along her spine until he stood behind her and could slip both hands around to her front. He covered both breasts with sure fingers, catching each nipple between the V of his index and middle fingers. Then he scissored them gently, squeezing her firm flesh, and flattened the front of his body along the back of hers.

She felt his hard cock pressing into her fanny and knew he must have helped himself out of his trousers. She wanted to reach behind herself and stroke him, but what he was doing to her just felt too good for her to move from her position against the wall just yet. He continued to palm her breasts for several long moments, then moved his hands down over her flat torso and between her legs. After he stroked her a few more times with sure fingers, he pushed his mouth against her ear again and murmured, "You don't seem to be carrying anything dangerous, other than the obvious. So now I want you to turn down the bed and lie down on it."

Reluctantly—she was still having rather a good time, after all—Rosie dropped her hands to her sides and turned around. Her pulse quickened and her anticipation leaped to the fore again when she saw Sam, his eyes dark with his passion, his cheeks flushed with his arousal, his clothes in disarray and his cock springing free of his trousers. After kissing him deeply and thoroughly for one long moment, she moved to the bed, handed him the cuffs still lying atop it, and began to turn it down. But she felt the heat of his gaze as she did so, and knew he was watching closely every move she made. She also heard the steady—and very erotic—clink…clink…clink…of the handcuffs as he waited for her to finish.

A little explosion of heat spread through her belly as she lay down on the bed and looked up at him. It fired through her like a rocket when he smiled and told her, "Roll over."

Smiling, her heart pounding now, she turned onto her stomach, then, at his direction, lifted her hands over her head, toward the headboard. A shudder of excitement shook her at the sound of the handcuffs—*chink, chink*—locking over her head. She thought he would finish undressing and join her, but he went to his closet instead. When he returned, he was holding a necktie in each hand.

"One hundred percent silk," he told her. "I've never worn either of them. Don't even know why I ever bought them, really. Always thought they were a waste of money." He grinned. "Until now." He glanced down at her feet, then back at her face. "But only if you're okay with it," he added.

For all her sexual adventurousness, Rosie had never been bound at every extremity before. She'd never allowed it. But suddenly, she found herself warming to the idea. More than warming. She was getting hotter than she'd ever been before at the prospect of having Sam tie her up. Because she trusted him completely and knew he would keep her safe. Totally safe and incredibly aroused. What better combination could there be?

Slowly, she nodded. "Oh, yeah," she said. "I'm more than okay with it. Way more than okay."

He smiled again, then went to the foot of the bed and wrapped a necktie loosely around each of her ankles. He pulled her legs wide and anchored both to the footboard, and then Rosie was well and truly helpless.

And, oh, did it feel good.

She watched as he finished undressing, his cock looking even harder and longer than usual, so he was clearly as aroused by this new adventure in passion as she was. For long moments, he only stood naked beside the bed watching her, taking himself in his hand and stroking himself slowly back and forth. Then he moved onto the mattress and knelt beside her head, and she opened her mouth so he could ease his cock inside.

He held on to the headboard as he moved his hips forward, pushing himself deeper and deeper into her mouth. Rosie's hands cuffed to the bed involuntarily jerked, because she wanted to hold that glorious length in her fingers as she sucked him. Since that was impossible, she opened her mouth wider in a silent bid for him to go deeper still.

Back and forth he moved his hips, pushing his cock in and out of her mouth, farther with every new foray. Since she couldn't use her hands, Rosie loved him with her tongue, twisting it around his head and licking it along his length. She groaned at the hunger building inside her, something that made Sam thrust even harder, even deeper. She sensed he was close to coming when he suddenly withdrew, but he bent to cover her mouth with his, kissing her with long, lingering strokes of his tongue.

Then he was moving on the bed again, opening his palms over her back and stroking her tender flesh, first her shoulders, then her nape, then her ribs, then her spine. Then he was rubbing his hands over her ass, pulling her cheeks apart and then pushing them together again, drawing a slow line down the crease before pushing his thumb gently inside her. Rosie cried out in pleasure, the sound doubling when he moved his other hand between her legs and began to plow his fingers through the hot flesh of her sex. For a long time, he only knelt beside her, fingering her body with both hands. He pushed his fingers into and out of her, threaded them through the wet folds of her skin, fondled, caressed, stroked and penetrated her.

And all the while, Rosie could only lie still and let him have his way. Although her hands and feet jerked at their bonds, she remained wide-open to his onslaught and was helpless to stop him. Not that she wanted to stop him. Mostly she wanted to join him in touching herself. But Sam knew even better than she what gave her the most pleasure. And he took his time giving it to her.

She didn't know how many times she came before he finally positioned himself behind her with his hands braced on the mattress beside both her hips. But she felt his cock rubbing against her, then pushing between her legs, then finally easing inside her. Deep, deep, deep inside her. Again she yanked at the cuffs and ties holding her down, and again she was overcome by arousal when she realized she was at Sam's mercy. He drilled her slowly at first, taking his time moving his big cock in and out of her. Gradually, though, his pace quickened and he rocked his hips harder against her. They came as one, crying out their release, then Sam slumped over her, spent.

After several long moments, he moved again, this time to free her from her bonds and the cuffs. Rosie rolled over to look at him, loving him more than she'd thought possible. Weakly, she raised her arms to him. This time when he joined her on the bed, it was to simply hold her close, until they fell into a quiet slumber. But a few hours later, they awoke to darkness, wanting each other all over again.

This time Rosie took the initiative, rolling Sam onto his back. Facing away from him, she straddled him to position herself on all fours, then lowered her head to his cock. But he must have had the same idea, because as she drew his cock into her mouth, he gripped her hips and pulled her backward until her tender flesh was hovering over his face. As she sucked him, she felt his tongue flicking against her damp folds, and her fingers clenched tighter around him. She felt his hands on her ass, rubbing and stroking and caressing, and she waited for that exquisite additional penetration she'd come to love. As if he'd heard her speak the thought aloud, he pushed his thumb inside her where she'd wanted it, burying it to the base. Rosie sucked him in deeper to show her gratitude, pushing the head of his cock against the roof of her mouth, then to the back of her throat.

She sucked him and he licked her, lapping his tongue over her sensitive wet flesh until she felt the coil of her climax growing tight in her belly. She released him from her mouth but continued to run her tongue up and down the length of him, circling the head with the tip before giving it a little nibble. Sam hissed his delight in response, then increased his own rhythm, stabbing her clit with his tongue and penetrating her ass with his thumb again and again and again.

When she knew she was ready to come, she levered herself off of him, and turned around, but before she could straddle him, Sam had her flat on her back, gripping her ankles in his strong fingers. He pulled her legs apart, spreading them in a wide V, then knelt before her and thrust his cock deep inside her. He pulled her halfway off the bed as he slammed into her, draping her legs over his shoulders to drive himself deeper still. Rosie cried out at the intensity of her orgasm, then felt Sam's hot release right behind it.

Exhausted and finally, finally, spent, they collapsed side by side on the bed. Sam tugged Rosie close and enfolded her in his arms, tucking her head beneath his chin. His heart hammered against hers, his skin as hot and damp as her own.

It would always be this way between them, she thought. They would always make love as if it were the last chance they might have to be together, even knowing they would never be apart again. They both knew too well how quickly things could disappear, and they knew better than anyone not to take anything for granted.

But she also knew Sam would always be there for her, just as she would be there for him. They would spend the rest of their lives together and grow old in this house in Northaven. He would protect her from the dangers of the world, and she would protect him from its ugliness. Their journey would be filled with more joy than she ever could have imagined, and they would weather what few bumps might occur in the road because they had each other.

From here on out, Sam Maguire would be her only vice. Her biggest virtue. And the man she loved forever.

* * * * *

Set in darkness beyond the ordinary world.
Passionate tales of life and death.
With characters' lives ruled by laws the everyday
world can't begin to imagine.

Introducing NOCTURNE, *a spine-tingling new line*
from Silhouette Books.

The thrills and chills begin with UNFORGIVEN by
Lindsay McKenna

Plucked from the depths of hell, former military sharp-shooter Reno Manchahi was hired by the government to kill a thief, but he had a mission of his own. Descended from a family of shape-shifters, Reno vowed to get the revenge he'd thirsted for all these years. But his mission went awry when his target turned out to be a powerful seductress, Magdalena Calen Hernandez, who risked everything to battle a potent evil. Suddenly, Reno had to transform himself into a true hero and fight the enemy that threatened them all. He had to become a Warrior for the Light....

Turn the page for a sneak preview of UNFORGIVEN
by Lindsay McKenna.
On sale September 26, wherever books are sold.

Chapter 1

One shot...one kill.

The sixteen-pound sledgehammer came down with such fierce power that the granite boulder shattered instantly. A spray of glittering mica exploded into the air and sparkled momentarily around the man who wielded the tool as if it were a weapon. Sweat ran in rivulets down Reno Manchahi's drawn, intense face. Naked from the waist up, the hot July sun beating down on his back, he hefted the sledgehammer skyward once more. Muscles in his thick forearms leaped and biceps bulged. Even his breath was focused on the boulder. In his mind's eye, he pictured Army General Robert Hampton's fleshy, arrogant fifty-year-old features on the rock's surface. Air exploded from between his lips as he brought the avenging hammer down. The boulder pulverized beneath his funneled hatred.

One shot...one kill...

Nostrils flaring, he inhaled the dank, humid heat and drew it deep into his massive lungs. Revenge allowed Reno to endure his imprisonment at a U.S. Navy brig near San Diego, California. Drops of sweat were flung in all directions as the crack of his sledgehammer claimed a third stone victim. Mouth taut, Reno moved to the next boulder.

The other prisoners in the stone yard gave him a wide berth. They always did. They instinctively felt his simmering hatred, the palpable revenge in his cinnamon-colored eyes, was more than skin-deep.

And they whispered he was different.

Reno enjoyed being a loner for good reason. He came from a medicine family of shape-shifters. But even this secret power had not protected him—or his family. His wife, Ilona, and his three-year-old daughter, Sarah, were dead. Murdered by Army General Hampton in their former home on USMC base in Camp Pendleton, California. Bitterness thrummed through Reno as he savagely pushed the toe of his scarred leather boot against several smaller pieces of gray granite that were in his way.

The sun beat down upon Manchahi's naked shoulders, grown dark red over time, shouting his half-Apache heritage. With his straight black hair grazing his thick shoulders, copper skin and broad face with high cheekbones, everyone knew he was Indian. When he'd first arrived at the brig, some of the prisoners taunted him and called him Geronimo. Something strange happened to Reno during his fight with the name-calling prisoners. Leaning down after he'd won the scuffle, he'd snarled into each of their bloodied faces that if they were going to call him anything, they would call him *gan,* which was the Apache word for *devil.*

His attackers had been shocked by the wounds on their faces, the deep claw marks. Reno recalled doubling his fist as they'd attacked him en masse. In that split second, he'd gone into an altered state of consciousness. In times of danger, he transformed into a jaguar. A deep, growling sound had emitted from his throat as he defended himself in the three-against-one fracas. It all happened so fast that he thought he had imagined it. He'd seen his hands morph into a forearm and paw, claws extended. The slashes left on the three men's faces after the fight told him he'd begun to shape-shift. A fist made bruises and swelling; not four perfect, deep claw marks. Stunned and anxious, he hid the knowledge of what else he was from these prisoners. Reno's only defense was to make all the prisoners so damned scared of him and remain a loner.

Alone. Yeah, he was alone, all right. The steel hammer swept downward with hellish ferocity. As the granite groaned in protest, Reno shut his eyes for just a moment. Sweat dripped off his nose and square chin.

Straightening, he wiped his furrowed, wet brow and looked into the pale blue sky. What got his attention was the startling cry of a red-tailed hawk as it flew over the brig yard. Squinting, he watched the bird. Reno could make out the rust-colored tail on the hawk. As a kid growing up on the Apache reservation in Arizona, Reno knew that all animals that appeared before him were messengers.

Brother, what message do you bring me? Reno knew one had to ask in order to receive. Allowing the sledge-hammer to drop to his side, he concentrated on the hawk who wheeled in tightening circles above him.

Freedom! the hawk cried in return.

Reno shook his head, his black hair moving against his broad, thickset shoulders. *Freedom? No way, Brother. No way.* Figuring that he was making up the hawk's shrill message, Reno turned away. Back to his rocks. Back to picturing Hampton's smug face.

Freedom!

Look for UNFORGIVEN by Lindsay McKenna,
the spine-tingling launch title from
Silhouette Nocturne™.
Available September 26, wherever books are sold.

nocturne™

Save $1.⁰⁰ off

**your purchase of any
Silhouette® Nocturne™ novel.**

Receive $1.00 off

any Silhouette® Nocturne™ novel.

**Available wherever books are sold, including most
bookstores, supermarkets, drugstores and discount stores.**

Coupon expires December 1, 2006. Redeemable at participating
retail outlets in the U.S. only. Limit one coupon per customer.

5 65373 00076 2   (8100) 0 11265

SNCOUPUS

Save $1.⁰⁰ off

your purchase of any
Silhouette® Nocturne™ novel.

Receive $1.00 off

any Silhouette® Nocturne™ novel.

**Available wherever books are sold, including most
bookstores, supermarkets, drugstores and discount stores.**

Coupon expires December 1, 2006. Redeemable at participating
retail outlets in Canada only. Limit one coupon per customer.

RETAILER: Harlequin Enterprises Limited will pay the face value of this coupon
plus 10.25 cents if submitted by the customer for this specified product only. Any
other use constitutes fraud. Coupon is nonassignable. Void if taxed, prohibited or
restricted by law. Consumer must pay any government taxes. Mail to Harlequin
Enterprises Ltd., P.O. Box 3000, Saint John, New Brunswick E2L 4L3, Canada. Limit
one coupon per customer. Valid in Canada only.

52607136

SNCOUPCDN

THE PART-TIME WIFE

by *USA TODAY* bestselling author

Maureen Child

Abby Talbot was the belle of Eastwick society;
the perfect hostess and wife. If only her
husband were more attentiive. But when
she sets out to teach him a lesson and files
for divorce, Abby quickly learns her husband's
true identity...and exposes them to scandals
and drama galore!

On sale October 2006 from Silhouette Desire!

*Available wherever books are sold,
including most bookstores, supermarkets,
discount stores and drug stores.*